BOOKS BY SKOOT LARSON

The Lars Lindstrom Zen Jazz Mystery series

The No News is Bad News Blues

The Real Gone Horn Gone Blues

The Dig You Later Alligator Blues

The On the Road Again Blues

The Dave Holman "Texas" Mystery series

The Texas Detective

The Pachyderm Predicament

Political Humor

Apollo Issue, a Humorous Look at Healthcare

The Palestine Solution

The Testament of Jessica Crystal

A humorous novel by
Skoot Larson

Skoot's
Jazz
Books

Rockport, Texas

ISBN: 13: 978-0-692-67106-1

Published by Skoot's Jazz Books

Rockport, Texas

"One day the people that didn't believe will tell everyone how they met you"

— Johnny Depp

"Blasphemy is a victimless crime"

— Richard Dawkins

PROLOGUE

Mary couldn't sleep. She kept having this feeling that her life just wasn't going anywhere. Sure, her boyfriend, Joseph, was a nice enough guy, a real stand-up guy, but she just didn't feel any chemistry there. It was just so frustrating.

"I'm know I'm meant for something more than this!" she kept telling herself as she went up on the roof of their boxy desert hut to stare into the overhead stars. Joseph lay downstairs in their bed snoring louder than a plague of locusts.

Then, from out of the night sky, a brilliant light appeared and continued to approach her and glow ever brighter. Mary blinked twice and the light began to take the shape of a woman standing before her, but standing on what? This woman shimmered on the warm desert air! And then she spoke.

"Listen, Mary. I know you'll find this hard to believe…Sometimes I almost don't believe it myself, but really, this was too important for me to trust it to a band of angels or something to give you the edict!"

Mary stood in awe, too breathless to speak. Her jaw was resting on the slope of her ample chest and she couldn't seem to bring it back far enough for her lips to meet and form words.

"Alright, already, so you might have guessed it," said a voice like Joan Rivers, "I'm God and we need to talk! Can we talk?"

The figure before Mary looked a lot like Ella Fitzgerald, but Mary couldn't have recognized her as such because it would be another two thousand years before God recreated the greatest of all jazz singers in her own image.

"Mary," God continued, "are you listening to me? Your eyes look kinda glassy. Have you been smoking that...?"

"Ah, oh... what?" stammered the poor girl.

"You know the Rabbis have been talking about a savior? Someone to give salvation to all the children of Israel?"

Mary slowly and mechanically nodded her head.

"Well... I have chosen *you*." God laid a fifty-thousand candle power smile on the confused girl. "***You*** are going to give birth to the savior!" God showed her a smug and happy face with lots of bright, white teeth.

"S-s-savior?" Mary repeated, like a slow parrot. "Birth to a savior?"

"You got it, Sweetie! Listen, it has *got* to be a virgin birth so everyone will believe!"

"Virgin? But... Oh God! You must know that I've..."

"Oy, virgin smirgin, you got a good reputation? The town doesn't gossip about you foolin' around. That guy you're seeing, Joseph? He actually *complains* to his friends that he's not getting any! So I think you'll do nicely!"

"But what if... I mean? Oh oy! Why me God?"

A coffee-colored hand reached out of the night and patted Mary's hand. "You think God would steer you wrong? Just play along with me! A thousand years from now, the whole world will still be speaking your name! You'll be bigger than a rock star... Oh, sorry, I guess that doesn't mean a lot to you at this point in time, but trust me, I know what I'm doing!"

I

It wasn't quite a year later that Joseph had to go out of town on business, something to do with taxes and a census. Joseph invited Mary to travel with him, though he wasn't sure why. He *did* enjoy her company, and he had all these wild fantasies about her, but as much charm as he turned on, she remained about as warm as a plate of yesterday's Kugle.

Maybe if he popped the question, she'd warm up to him. He'd try that as they traveled through some exotic locale. She seemed to be putting on weight lately, almost as though they already *were* married.

The trip turned out to be a total disaster. The Hebrew Inns along the hot and dusty were all booked with conventions or something. A few nights in the park proved worthless for making any time, but finally, the Howard Johnstein in the berg of Bethlehem had something better for them.

It was a small, semi-private room in the stables, but their neighbors would be mostly asses and other farm animals. Joseph signed the guest register and then rubbed his hands together with a leer in his eye.

But their semi-secluded accommodations proved no joy. "Can't you just let me sleep?" Mary begged him.

"I'm just so tired of humping and hand jobs," Joseph snapped back at her. "I want to start a serious family!"

"Oh, Joseph," Mary answered, "We can't do that now. God told me I'm about to give birth to the savior of the people of Israel. It has to be a virgin birth, I'm so sorry!"

"Virgin birth!" Joseph exploded. "Hah! It's probably my son! They way the flies move around on these dry desert nights!"

"But it may not *be* a *son*," Mary cooed. "After all, God is…"

"A savior that isn't a son?" Joseph exploded. "Have you been listening to those Egyptian refugees again? Those folks with their lady Sun God?"

Joseph was awakened some hours later to the sound of trumpets in the sky. His eyes blinked open to a light brighter than day and he turned to see Mary with an infant in her arms.

"Huh?" he managed.

"It's the savior," Mary replied smugly. "Just as God promised!"

Joseph rolled over and grabbed the child, holding it close to him.

"Yes," he exclaimed. "It *is* the son of God!"

"It's a girl," Mary scolded. "And please let go of my finger!"

Jan 21, 2018

Dear Geoff + Darla,

Greetings from Rockport, TX. I am loving life here in this small Gulf town. The energy is incredible!! The unity is small and very "aware" with a very warm pastor. Her name is Carolyn. She was in Houston prior to being here (since Oct, 2017 shortly after the Hurricane Harvey). I have made many friends and Scott is one of them. He wrote the book I'm sending you (read it as "humor" - or maybe not). Anyway after I read it you guys kept coming to mind. I hope you enjoy it. Scott has also written many other books and his mystery (I just finished) take place in Rockport.

Love to you and all of my Tulsa friends,
Cathy

II

Not being so heartless as to send a couple with a newborn out into the streets, the innkeeper had offered Joseph a job shoveling out the stables, which would cover the rent, the inn's buffet breakfast and dinner off the set menu in the hotel's falafel stand. All the while, the strange light of what appeared to be some large star shown down upon them all.

And throughout all this time, not another word from God, although Mary had great faith that the woman was still there for them. She held Joseph at bay telling him that she thought she *might* be a lesbian. Being a bit homophobic, Joseph hung back from her, sleeping with the donkey in the next stable each night. From the sound of things, Mary began to think that Joseph had finally found a mate more suited to him.

On the fifth week of Savior Jessica's life, three bearded hep-cats wearing Shriner-style fezzes arrived at the manger bearing colorfully wrapped packages covered with pictures of reindeer and some kind of bearded clown in a red suit. They rode into town on camels, which attracted some attention in and of itself. As they ducked their heads and rode their beasts into the stable proper, Joseph stood up to bar their way.

"What's the meaning of this intrusion?" he shouted. "What do you want with us?"

"The first camel-jockey smirked, "Hey, we're the wise guys!"

"*Men,*" said the gent on the last camel. "We're wise *men*! We ain't here from Sicily! Don't get me started on this!"

"Anyway," added the middle camel jockey, "we've been following that really heavy, wigged-out, psychedelic star up there. What a trip! Like this really hep lady who said she was *God* told us we needed to bring some gifts to the party. Like, uh, myrrh and Lincoln-sense"

"That's Frankincense, you idiot," the first man cut in. "Haven't you been paying attention?"

"So why the camels?" Mary asked. "Donkey's ain't good enough for you?"

"Good enough for us?" the third man stated. "Listen, this God lady told us we needed to make a *statement* here, we're supposed to be part of a big historic show. She guaranteed us a cameo in some kinda Holy book!"

"I thought we should rent elephants," the first wise man told her. "Do you know how much Budget Rentals charges to hire an elephant for a week? A camel is bad enough! Three elephants would have set us back half a year's tax revenue. And try explaining *that* to a population that thinks taxes are too high and we're indulging ourselves already… I mean even if this kid of yours really *does* turn out to be a messiah or something!"

His buddy's camel sidled up next to him and the third wise man elbowed him in the ribs. "Hey, watch it, *pal*. We don't want to piss Ms. God off, do we?"

Both the other wise guys… er, men shook their head back and forth. Camel jockey one took their hint.

"So…" Mary asked, "You've brought me some kind of incense and spices? When you never even asked if I could cook? Even *Joseph*

-8-

knows I have trouble boiling water. You couldn't have brought disposable diapers or some kind of germicidal-wipes? Do you know the kind of parasites that breed in this climate?

Joseph nodded his head in the background. He was sure this lesbian thing that had a grip on his Mary came from some kind of desert weavel. He regularly read those Fox News tablets that were left in the inn's lobby and believed every word of their reporting. He couldn't wait to get these wise guys alone for an intimate discussion of his conspiracy theory about modern fool Rabbis! This black Ms. God was probably some sort of mass hallucination created by the ultra-liberal media trying to bring some kind of free-love socialist program to the children of Israel. The nerve of these people! Oh, the humanities! And free love? Where was *that* for him, anyway…?

"So, enough of this idle chit-chat," said the first wise man. "Where is this special kiddy we came all this way to see?"

Mary picked little Jessica up from her bed of straw and proudly held the infant out for her guests to praise. The men hung back for a few seconds, not sure just how to deal with such a historic situation, but Mary pushed the baby out towards them for their inspection.

The wise man closest to Mary reached out and took the little girl partly into his arms. "Oh wow, dig me, cats! I'm holdin' our savior!"

The second wise man reached out to the child as well. "Yeah, baby! It *is* the son of God!"

"Not you too," Mary frowned. "It's a *girl*. The child is a *girl*, so will you please let go of my finger!"

The extremely embarrassed wise man drew back, but then his face broke out in a warm smile. "This is too cool!" he told his buddies. "Better break out the jug. I think it's party time."

Joseph, in the mood to get a little toasted, nodded his head in agreement, but Mary gave them a confused look.

"It's not even lunch time yet. Isn't it a bit early to get all juiced up?"

"Lady, wait'll you hear the best part, then I think you'll be ready for a little happy grape juice yourself," smirked the third wise man. "Old King Harry, like, he's been hearing rumors, dig? When he heard we were headin' west to check out the wild star, he laid a very un-cool rap on us, sayin' if there really *is* a Son of God out there, he's gonna start killin' babies to protect his thrown from some Levantine kid takin' over."

"That's terrible," wailed Mary. "This is supposed to be good news?"

"The good news," said wise man one, "is that he's gonna be lookin' for a *male* child! Ol' Harry is far too conservative to entertain the idea of a female savior, so your little Jessica will be safe. Hey Isaac, have you found that jug yet?"

At this, Joseph looked up with terror in his eyes. "You guys ain't gonna rat us out are you? You're not here looking to blackmail us? We don't have any assets!"

Wise man two gave a hearty laugh as he pulled the gallon-sized ceramic jug of sauce out of his saddlebag along with five very hip little tea cups. "Are you kiddin' me? Old Harry is a *tyrant*. We don't have any love for him!"

"We're gonna take all the back roads home," added the first man, "Just so we don't have to deal with this kingly cat again. But, like, just to be cool, you guys might want to go hang out in Egypt for a season or three, in case his soldiers decide to kill little girls too. I wouldn't put anything past those sadistic guards in old Harry's army.

The wise men posed behind Jessica, Mary and Joseph in their humble stable for some painter who said he'd like to preserve the scene for posterity. The picture wasn't that great, the perspective was way off and the artist improvised some kind of flying women he said were supposed to be the angels one would expect at such an event.

At least his work would provide inspiration for later painters with more talent somewhere down the line. God herself explained it to Mary, although Mary was clueless about art and said it really didn't matter to her.

The party went on well into the night. The landlord of the stable, hearing their laughter, brought another jug of his own best red to the gathering. A good time was had by all and even Joseph was smiling as he tootled back to his bunk in the donkey's pen.

III

Late in the night Joseph was awakened by a lovely and rhythmic voice approaching his bed singing, "A tisket a tasket, a green and yellow basket, I wrote a letter to my God and on the way I dropped it…"

"Hark!" young Joseph called out in surprise, "who goes there." The donkey at his side awoke with a soft, low bray.

"Well you can see I ain't no Playboy bunny," laughed God. "It's just me dropping by to lay it on you that those wise guys know their stuff. It's close to time for you to take Mary and the kid and split for Egypt. The more of a lead you get on King Harry, the better. And I just happen to have a recent Union Oil map you can follow to find the quickest route out of town."

Never very good with authority figures, Joseph wasn't sure how to respond. He shifted his weight from one foot to the other, 'emming and awing.

"Oh, come on, Joe, don't be shy," the dark shimmering lady told him. "Mary speaks quite highly of you, and I personally know you ain't no dummy… Hell, I created you, like I did all the other players in this crazy little show."

"Egypt?" Joseph managed to squeak, "Anywhere special in Egypt?"

"Your call, big fellah," God told him. "I hear the beach outside Alexandria is nice, but the important thing is to avoid King Harry and his minions until I give you the all clear."

"You give me the all clear," Joseph parroted in a dazed tone.

"Hey, I'm everywhere," God chuckled. "No problem finding you wherever you go!" She gave him a lecherous wink, then began to fade.

"Wait," Joseph shouted, "don't you need to talk to Mary or something?"

God regained some substance for half a minute and gave Joseph a big grin. "Mary understands," she told him. "And pretty soon that girl you're raising will be explaining a *lot more* to you and *all* the people of Israel."

Joseph had always been a good boy. He tried to get to Torah study every Saturday and he always respected his elders. He never gazed lustfully on any of the *Jewish* girls, apart from Mary, who was his wife of record at least.

Of course, the shiksas were something else! Boy could those babes get him hot, but that was okay. The Ten Commandments only applied to his own tribe of Hebrew people. Shiksas were fair game.

He slept fitfully after God left his bedside. Even counting Shiksas jumping a fence that he was lying under to look up their robes couldn't seem to bring him any peace. He finally decided to get out of bed and start packing. Egypt couldn't be any worse than this little four-corners where he had become stuck by the sudden birth of an unexpected daughter. And he'd have his favorite donkey, Molly, with him wherever they went. That, at least, was a comfort.

When Mary awoke for the child's two-o'clock feeding, Joseph laid the plan out for her. They would take the two-lanes marked on

Mother God's Union Oil map and avoid the main highways across the Sinai. Once in Egypt, they'd rent a small place in an unpretentious little suburb where they wouldn't attract too much attention.

Mary agreed, but in her heart she knew their young Jessica was going to be a real handful. God's daughter, she feared, would find a way to glean attention no matter where they went!

And Mary wasn't wrong! When young Jessica didn't want to take a bath, she would simply walk on the water in the tub, refusing to immerse herself. How could she do that? Well, she was the daughter of God, but still!

And when Mary served corned beef, Jessica would often turn up her nose at the cow carcass and turn her steak into a plate of fish. A very difficult child!

Young Jessica was such a precocious child that Mary was afraid to take her out in public for fear the girl would embarrass her by putting mustaches on the neighborhood ladies, or turning their fine robes into skimpy nightwear. "Oh Mother God," she cried out. "What have you blessed me with?"

But Jessica was basically a good kid. She respected all those worthy of her respect and only played tricks on the people who thought themselves above their peers. As soon as she was old enough to understand, Jessica spent her Saturdays at the Rabbi's feet in an old Egyptian synagogue, gleaning all she could about the faith of her ancestors. She studied the Torah and asked all the right questions of the Rabbis, until her questions became too much for these temple teachers to handle; questions about the universe and why one tribe of people should be held above another.

Jessica wasn't exactly kicked out of the temple, but the Rabbis made it pretty clear that their job was easier when this curious child didn't show up. Joseph would tell them that Jessica should not be excluded as, on his side of the family, she was a direct descendent of King David, so many times removed, but the Rabbis would argue that Jessica's virgin birth removed her from such lineage. It was a standoff as neither side would give in, so Jessica would sneak into the back row of Torah study and just take notes. If she really needed answers, she could always check with Mother God.

IV

Mother Mary tried to teach her young daughter girly things like cooking and sewing, but the child had a short span of interest, maybe even ADHD. Jessica fidgeted and fussed and wouldn't sit still. Most sessions ended in a frustrated Mary sending the girl out in the yard to play with the farm animals.

On one afternoon, when following Jessica outside Mary found the girl staring fascinated at Joseph and his team of men building a tract of new houses down the block. Jessica was asking some pretty good questions about load-bearing walls and door lintels.

The lead builder, a Mr. Levitt, was happy to show the young girl all the tricks to his trade, remarking to Joseph that he thought Jessica would make a fine carpenter.

"But girls aren't carpenters," a distraught Mary told the man upon overhearing their conversation. "Girls must learn to cook and sew so they can find a good husband to support and take care of them!"

Mr. Levitt laughed. "I'd learn to cook and sew if I had such a girl as this to run my building business. With a girl like this, I could construct Levitt towns all over the Sinai in record time!"

Mother Mary dragged her daughter back inside for now, but there was no way she could keep the girl away from the local construction sites. Before she knew it, Jessica had acquired a leather belt with rings and holsters for her own hammer, saw, level and measuring tape. Mary threatened the local tradesmen that she would turn them in for violating child labor laws but, this being the year 7 AD no one paid her much attention.

Mary and Joseph were extremely thankful when God came to their small cold-water flat outside Cairo to tell them it was safe to return to Israel.

"Anyplace special in Israel?" Joseph asked, unfolding the Union Oil map God had laid on him some years before.

"Actually," God told him with a pensive look, "yeah, I think a little berg called Nazareth would be a good choice."

"Nazareth?" replied Mary and Joseph in unison.

"Yes!" Mother God hissed. It looks like a nice neighborhood... And they can call young Jessie a 'Nazarene! That has a very memorable ring to it! I like that! Nazarene!"

"Nazarene," the young Jessica's parents repeated as though in a trance.

"Yes!" Jessica shouted behind them raising two clenched fists. "I'm going to be *The **Nazz**!*"

V

"We're supposed to be on holiday here, dear." Mother Mary scolded her daughter. "Old Joe brought us down to the beach to relax. Can't you just relax? You should get your towel out and catch some rays, dear. What can you gain with all this pacing about?"

"Vacation? God blind me," young Jessica cursed. "What a God forsaken bit of fucking desert! There's simply nothing here. No night life, no intellectual people to interact with. I *hate* this place! They don't even have a decent coffee house!"

"Now dear…" Mary said looking up from her sewing. "I don't think God appreciates your vulgar language! After all, you're only ten years old!"

"Oh yeah, *God*." Jessica closed her eyes and shook her head. "Galilee, Jesse Crystal! I thought she said *Galway*. A holiday in Galway!"

"Now you know you shouldn't take *your* name in vain, sweetie. Galway?"

"Yeah, Galway. It's a town in Ireland."

"Ireland?"

"Oh, you wouldn't understand. God, why is everyone so dense around here?"

"Dense?"

"Dense! As in thick as two short Greek columns! *Mother* Mary, Galway is a town in Ireland. Ireland is populated with *Celtic* people… Celtic people who have some soul! They have music you can dance to. They play music on harps and whistles and bagpipes!"

"Bagpipes?"

"No, you wouldn't get it! I tell you, as soon as I'm old enough I'm gonna twist God's arm about letting me wander around the world for some thirty years or so! Maybe, if I walk far enough from here, I might discover some intelligent life!"

"Intelligent life?"

"Forget it, Mother Mary." Jessica gave her earth mother a hug. "Maybe I can get God to explain some of it to you one day."

"That would be nice," Mary said, rolling her eyes toward heaven and wondering about her daughter's sanity.

Jessica walked out into the gathering gloom of desert nightfall. "Mother God," she pleaded in a sort of prayer, "why are you making this so tough for me!"

A glow materialized beside her. "Listen, already," came the voice even before the large dark skinned woman shimmered into view. "You want easy? You're supposed to be a savior to a whole race of people and you need some simple zip-zot! Someone to hold your hand? Oy, the youth of today!"

"Well," Jessica pondered.

"Hey, I'm God, okay? I know all and see all, right? Listen, stick with me on this and in a year or so I'll teach you some real fun stuff! How about I show you how to turn water into wine! No grapes or nothing! And good stuff too, none of this Mogen David 20/20 or Manischewitz Concord Grape crap! Something *drinkable* that the proletarians will go for!"

"But these peasants are all into *fish*!" Jessica protested. "I abhor white wine! I prefer that Dago red the Roman soldiers bring with them!"

"You naughty girl!" God tsked. "You've been hanging with those Roman soldiers?"

"Hey, Mother God!" Jessica scoffed. "They always treat me like a lady! And they're a lot more worldly then the local rubes!"

"Right! Hey, you're like, ten years old! They damn well better treat you…"

"Yeah, except that Caesar guy! I don't like the way he looks at me…."

"He's been leering at you, Jessica? I'll fix his little I-tye butt! I'll have to give him epilepsy or something. Remind me to make a note…"

"Oh Mother God! Can you blame him? I *am* a cute little package!" Jessica wiggled her butt and smiled at God.

"Yes, a ten-year-old package! There's no excuse for short-eyes like that. Damn politicians! Think they can get away with anything!

"Tell you what kid," God confided. "I'm gonna give you a few lessons in temptation. I'm gonna send you out into some wilderness, a secluded forest or something for oh, I don't know, maybe forty days will do it."

"We have forests around here?" Jessie countered.

"Well, alright already. Maybe I'll have to send you up to Lebanon or someplace."

"Why not Ireland?" Jessica queried, full of hope.

"Not that much wilderness," Mother God told her. "Listen, already. You're going into this forest and fast for forty days, then I'm going to send some temptations your way."

"Oh, could you? I just love **My Girl**…and **Get Ready**!"

"Hold on, child!" God scolded. "I don't mean that vocal group from somewhere way in the future. I mean like some kinda good-time Joe, some devil type that will try and *tempt* you to act bad; to not conduct yourself like a proper lady!"

"Oh, that sounds like fun!" Jessie cooed with a wide grin.

"But you've gotta *resist* these temptations," Mother God laid on her in an exasperated tone. "This is all part of showing the proles that you're really the daughter of God."

"Oh, alright. I could use a bit of fasting. I seem to be putting on a few extra pounds lately…."

God rolled her eyes toward heaven. "I created this young lady to be a world savior? Too much in my own image," she scolded herself.

VI

Little Jessica grew, mentally far faster than physically, although she was maturing pretty quickly. By twelve years old, Jessica was becoming quite a hot little item as well as being filled with the wisdom and grace of Mother God. Jessica had long raven hair and dark soulful eyes over a body most young women would sell their souls to have, but to Jessica, it was nothing special. She thought of her intellect as her most prized possession.

Mary and Old Joseph made it a thing to go to Jerusalem every spring for the feast of Passover, although it wasn't much of a feast with all the dietary restrictions. In this particular year, Jessica celebrated her twelfth birthday and so had her Bat Mitzvah as well. It was a lengthy celebration and when it was over Jessica, now reaching adulthood in the eyes of the temple, didn't show up in time for the caravan back home. Mary and Joseph were, like, clueless!

When they'd checked out all the local hot spots and hadn't turned up their little lady, they dug that she must be hanging out with some of the kin around the town. They spent some time going back and forth on a search, because who knew what kind of mischief a young girl of twelve could get into on her own.

After half a week of checkin' out all the spots, they found their girl in the temple, of all places. Jessica was sitting cross-legged on the temple floor, surrounded by all the local Rabbis, both listening to their rap and questioning them about their faith. All the cats and kitties who had made this scene were amazed at Jessica's understanding of the faith and the answers she offered to them.

When her parents saw her here they were gassed! Mary exclaimed, "Baby, why have you treated us like this? Like, we were really drug with all our fear about what could have happened to you."

"So why were you trying to cling on to my coat tails?" Jessica smiled. "I am officially a grown-up now. Couldn't you dig that Mother God was keeping an eye on me? And that I had to be doing her business while I was here?"

Being kind of lame from square one, Mary and Joseph couldn't get a handle on what their girl was laying down, but they kinda dug that she had some solid connections, so they just smiled and let it be.

And Jessica continued to cop more wisdom as Mother God shone through her young self.

VII

Within a few years, true to her word, God guided Jessica to a dark and secluded mountainous forest somewhere in the north. Jesse suspected it was Lebanon because of all the cedars, but God wasn't about to reveal her true location.

When they were settled in this remote wooded land quite a distance from the main highway, God found her a clear little stream feeding a small shaded pool.

"You're fasting now, Kid," God told her. "No cheating. You can drink all you want from the stream; in fact I recommend that you drink a lot. It'll help you to flush the poisons and bad jazz from your system. But you're not to eat anything! No mushrooms or truffles or plants like that! When you get depressed or hungry, just lay back in the water and do some meditations!"

"Oh, very vouty," replied the young savior. "This should be a piece of cake! And when it's over, I hope you'll send me a piece of cake... and a big plate of baba ganoush as well!"

"Just keep your mind on fasting for now," God told her. "Try not to think about food and don't worry about the next chapter. You'll be going through some temptations, but I know you can handle it!"

"Because it will be easy?" Jesse asked.

"Because you're the savior of your people!" God replied emphatically. "Because you don't have any choice, young lady!"

Jessica got through the forty days meditating on what a hot little body she'd have after all that time of zero calories. She almost totally forgot about the temptations that were set to follow. On day forty-one, she emerged from her little shaded copse to search for some enticing roots or berries.

Approaching the distant highway, she saw a candy-apple red chariot with wire wheels and a lot of chrome trim. Beside the chariot was an obese Roman cat in a red cashmere toga and a gray felt stingy-brim fedora reclining on a blanket in the grass. As he tipped his sky-piece to her, she noticed that his ears were kind of pointy.

"Oh, hey baby!" he breathed on seeing Jessica emerge from the forest. He took a deep toke on a fat spliff and held it out to Jesse.

Jessica took the joint and inhaled a long puff. "What's happenin', Jackson," she grinned.

"*You* are happenin'," grinned the hep cat, "over and over! Man, you've got to be the finest little piece of tail I've ever seen!"

Jessica blushed. "Don't hand me none of your jive, daddy" she told him, "'cause I've heard it all before!"

"Oh no, it's not like that," the Roman hipster told her doing a serious face. "I'm on your side! I just thought that we could make a scene! I mean, I got eyes!"

"Yes, you certainly do," Jesse replied. "And they appear to be green with lust or envy, both of which I'm against, but that ain't *my* scene anyway, daddy. I just finished forty days like, without any food. Love is *not* what I'm lookin' to cop here!"

"That's cool, sweetie," said the big bad Roman devil. "So how about I barbeque us up a little lamb or something?"

"Meat is murder," Jesse replied, taking another hit from the joint. "I don't have eyes for any dead animals. You got any eggplant, or some curried chick peas? I'm starving!"

The hipster made a face and looked away. "If it's your sexy little *physical body* you want to feed, I can fix you up with some really groovy and worthy studs" he offered, "Handsome boys that will simply rock your world!"

"My world just kinda rocks on its own," Jessica smiled. "Now about those veggies…."

"Veggies," the Roman repeated disdainfully, then he brought a small folded square of waxed parchment from the pocket of his robe. "How about we do a little blow?" he asked, unfolding the small package.

"Again, not my thing," Jessica told him pulling her robe tighter around her as she gave a little shiver.

"Oh, right, like you're this savior chick. I dig! So show me something from your bag of tricks. I got a big pile of very cool round stones here. How about you turn them into loaves of bread for me?"

"Man can't live by bread alone," Jessica told him. "Besides, bread from a stone would be heavier than mother Mary's biscuits! I prefer a nice braided *challah* with sweet poppy seeds!"

"Oh yeah, right… Well how about you hop in my fine red ride and we head for the temple? I want to do a thing with you!"

"As long as it doesn't involve me getting' close to that rancid breath of yours!"

The rotund Roman popped a couple hard candy mints in his mouth, then continued. "Hey, baby! Trust me on this. I just gotta check up on a religious matter or two. There's some egg salad sandwiches in the basket there, maybe a tuna as well, so you don't waste away on the drive."

Their chariot sped down the mountain into a town. Jessica was kind of digging the breeze flowing through her hair and freshening her froozy robe that had only been rinsed in the stream for more than a month. The Roman was a really bad driver, but if you've ever driven in Rome, you'll know this is pretty typical. At least the roads were clear and there wasn't too much traffic. The chariot was a very smooth ride, even if a bit ostentatious. They were getting some solid looks of envy from the few peasants that they passed.

The Roman cat parked illegally in a handicapped spot near the main entrance to the temple. Jessica thought about putting a serious hurt on him to justify his parking there, but dismissed it as, in her heart, she really wanted one of the local cops to give him a hefty citation for his audacity.

She followed the man up two flights of stairs and a shaky ladder that put them on the roof of the building.

"Alright, baby-cakes," the Roman smiled at her. "So you are supposed to be this big Levantine savior chick. They say that you've got this heavenly connection and that God has your back. So I want you to jump over the side! I'll be watching for all these angels and cherubs that are gonna catch you before you hit the bricks!"

"Listen, I think that, like, you're this devil cat Mother God has been telling me about!"

The Roman cat started to turn very red and steam poured forth from his ears. "You better be careful with that shit," he shouted. "I've got some very good connections! I could sue your tight little ass into the next…"

"Don't think so!" Jesse laughed. "I hereby banish you from my presence. Get lost, clown! I ain't doing some flying Ariel act so you can get your rocks off!"

At which point, the fat Roman cat morphed into Mother God.

"Congratulations, Jessica," God beamed at her. "You passed your temptations with high marks… but I'm a little disappointed in your toking so much reefer."

"It's cool." Jessica answered. "Hey, it's all natural and organic!"

Mother God rolled her eyes toward heaven, but said no more.

VIII

J essica shook her head at all these temptation things. Why did Mother God need to lay all these tests on her? But then again, she was God, so there must be a good reason.

Reading her thoughts, God shimmered down to the road in front of her. "Listen, kid, I'm known for working in mysterious ways my works to perform, okay? Are you cool with that?"

Jessica nodded that she dug it. After all, she was an intelligent girl, and she was having a pretty good adventure following God's instruction so far.

"So, you're God, but you can be this devil guy too?" Jesse inquired. "How does *that* work?"

God smiled. "I'm *it*, kid, all of it, the genuine all knowing, all seeing, all being article!"

"Well, I know you're the God of the Hebrew people…"

"Girl, I am **God**, the one and only! Other tribes and cultures might have other names for me and I answer to them all, but I truly am the only one out there. I *am the Lady*, your God and you can't go out, like, and choose another cause there ain't any other. To the folks up north, I'm a hairy plunderer, to the folks in the East, I'm a thousand droplets of water flowing in a calm and serene stream. To the Celts, I'm the Maiden of Spring, the Earth Mother…. I am spirit just as I am the sun, the moon and all the creatures that be!

"I'll let you in on a little secret, girl. Borders and tribes are just made up things… made up by people, *not* by me. There's really only one people, one tribe in this universe. We're all one, and my biggest job is to try and get people to understand this. We're all brothers and sisters and all come from the same source."

"That makes sense," Jessica said softly.

"Damn right it makes sense," God thundered a little too loudly. "And listen, this story about a garden and a bad snake? Well, that one was made up by men too. I tried to explain the world to this Ibrahim guy some years back, just like I'm telling you now, and next thing you know he's spreading this tale about women coming from some man's rib. He should get a good ribbing for that, no pun intended!

"Anyway I'm the one God, so I'm all the Gods and all people are the same to me. Part of your job here is to spread the word for me; spread *my* word of peace, love and light, that all men should love their brothers and sisters and treat each other with respect! Treat each other like, well, like *Gods!*"

Jessica closed her eyes momentarily touching three fingers to her forehead.

"That's the key word here, respect. Show respect for everyone, whether they have a little or a lot. All of the people, no matter what tribe they profess to belong in, need to help everyone else. Share your blessing! Do all you can to lessen anyone else's suffering. Are you getting all this? The fasting, the temptations? It was all to prepare you to bring my message of peace and love to the world! To wound any one of my people is to wound all of my people!"

God's words seemed to fill Jessica with a warm, bright light. Suddenly, she realized that she was so much more than a smart girl with a hot little body. It dawned upon her that she had the power within her to heal the sick and to make people listen to and believe her. God's power was filling her to bursting! She opened her eyes to find the dark lady tapping her foot and staring her down.

"So I got this rube, John, who thinks we need some kind of ritual to make all this believable. Do you think you could stop by the river Jordan on your way home? Just let this guy hold your head under the water for a few seconds and tell him he's cool."

Jessica agreed, but when she arrived at the river bank, the cat that introduced himself as John wanted Jesse to hold *his* head under the water!

Where do we find all these kinky buggers? Jessica thought to herself, but she did as she was asked with a smile. The man then announced he should be called The Baptist, which was okey-doky with Jessica, but she seriously wondered about the man's motives. Was he sincere or just hoping to play a bigger role in God's plan?

IX

Now in her late teens and filled with God's light, Jessica attracted a following of young men that would do anything just to share her intellectual company.

Taking a little side trip to Syria, Jesse stopped off to check out Caper City by the Sea. It was on the border land between Zee-Booty and No-Where Tali. Everywhere Jesse went, she would speak to small gatherings of people. She told all these cats and kitties just to be cool, 'cause the world is a vouty and happening place! Peace and love are the key. Love all your brothers and sisters! But she encountered a lot of nay-sayers along the way.

Jessica stopped for a glass of wine in a little beach bar on the shore of the Sea of Galilee. Just making conversation, Jessica mentioned what a happenin' place this mortal world was in her usual message of love and light.

A couple of dudes down the bar cocked an ear and sent a drink up to Jessica. Jessica smiled back at them and they moved a few barstools closer.

The first cat slipped her some skin. "Like, my name is Simon, but you can call me Peter, dig? And this is my brother cat, Andrew. He ain't got another handle."

"We're, like, fisher cats," Andrew told her. "But it's been kinda dead lately. These corporate cats the Romans are sponsoring are getting all the fish with their big flotilla of warships, so we don't stand a chance!"

"What a drag!" Jesse declared. "We gotta do something about this! You dudes are fishermen? How about helping me 'fish' for some human souls?"

Of course she had to explain it to them, but they were quick learners and easily coped to God's words.

After a couple more glasses of wine, Peter and Andrew vowed to ditch their nets and join Jessica in her ministry.

"You guys will be special to me," she told them. "You're my first real disciples."

"Like, what's a disciple?" Andrew asked.

"You know," Jessica improvised. "It's like the follower of a philosopher or teacher. Would you feel more comfortable if I called you Apostles?"

"Your choice, Ms. Jessica," Peter told her. "We're not that familiar with either handle."

"Apostles is what Mother God said I should call my closest circle of followers. It means you're one of the small band of twelve that I'm selecting to be teachers along with me."

"Gotcha!" Andrew exclaimed. "Lay the jam on us and we'll do the spreading!"

Then two more cats walked in and parked themselves just down the bar on the open stools vacated earlier by Peter and Andrew. These cats were fishermen as well and easily recognized as such by their yellow nor'easters.

"Johnny and Jimmy," Peter whispered. "They hang out their nets just like us."

Jessica sent a round down to them and pretty soon they moved to a table to form a small circle around her.

After digging Jessica's message of peace and love, the two new brothers voted to support her cause any way they could. Jesse invited them all to accompany her wherever she might go.

The four men dug that idea, and together they started an enthusiastic dialogue about what seemed to be wrong in the temple these days.

"Now dig it, fellahs," Jessica told them. "I haven't come here to *abolish* the temple or the laws of the prophets. Rather I've come to seek your aid in fulfilling all these laws! I mean like, to do it right, bright and totally tight!"

Some new arrivals in the drinking establishment sat down at the next table and started listening in on Jessica's conversation with her new found friends.

"So what do we have here?" proclaimed one of the newcomers, dressed in the robes of a minor government official, "Some liberal rabble who want to look down on the establishment and everybody in it?"

"Filthy hippies," mumbled a man standing behind him.

"Hey, it's not like that," Jessica told them with a somber face while pushing her chair back and standing. "I think you cats are the salt of the earth! Uh, but sometimes salt gets diluted, dig? It becomes tasteless, and not much good for seasoning food. If we lived up north in a colder clime, it might be good to throw out on the roads to melt ice so the chariots don't go sliding around out of control…"

By now, the entire group of officials were standing, surrounding Jessica and her friends' table. Jessica remained standing to face them, moving her head around to make eye contact with each man in turn.

"You know you dudes could be the light of the world if you'd just get your act together and show some respect for Mother God."

"Mother God," one of the men sneered. "I thought we fled from Egypt to get away from silly notions like *female* deities!"

"Dude, you had better get it together!" Jessica told him. "Jehovah, Yahweh, Isis, whatever you want to call her, God is a lady! So, believe it or not, you'd better wise up, let your light shine and give credit to Mother God!"

As her four disciples stared them down with un-frightened eyes, the men backed up and returned to their own table where Jessica could hear them discussing all the possibilities. She smiled at the thought that she might have planted seeds of doubt about their old, staid ideas.

As they were set to order another round, and send a round to the men at the next table as well, Jessica noticed the owner of the drinking establishment circulating the room clearing tables. She couldn't help but notice that the man was pouring wine from unfinished cups into an old wineskin at his side.

Jessica stood and grabbed the sleeve of the man's robe. "Mother God won't approve of this," she told him. "When you put good wine in old wineskins, they can burst and the wine spills down your apron and all over the floor. You should only put *new* wine in *new* wineskins, then both are preserved… And you should only be pouring fresh wine for your customers! Don't be such a cheap bastard trying to sell us someone else's cast off!"

X

As Jessica and her friends traveled the lands spreading the word of Mother God, they recognized others like them that were studs worthy of helping teach the people of Israel. Jessica trusted her instincts with each new potential apostle that she met. With each new teacher candidate that came along, the others would also vote with their eyes and Jessica would trust their opinions right up there with her own. In the marketplace, they met a hip cat named Bart and a kinda square, but cool dude called Thomas. From the *Givern*ment folks that had mocked them earlier at the bar in Galilee, a tax collector, Matthew, sought them out to apologize and ended up joining their little tribe.

Then they added another Jimmy, whom they called James and a solid with-it boy who was known as Thad. Rounding out the group, they copped another Simon, who did *not* want to be called Peter, and an anxious, nervous, red-faced fellow labeled Judas Carrot Top by his buddies, who kept repeating, "One day this dude is gonna blow his cool and explode all over everybody!"

On a little walk-about around Nazareth one afternoon, the group came upon a man twisted and bent over in pain.

"Jessica," one of the young men in her entourage frowned at her. "This cat is obviously suffering. Can't you call on this God woman you're always talking about and help this poor fellah?"

"Huh?" Jessica barked. "I don't need to bother God with this. I can handle it myself."

One of her cats, James, hurried over to the crippled old fellow and told him, "Be cool and stand by, my brother. I got someone here that's going to give you relief! You don't need to show this chick any cash or an insurance card or nothing!"

"A *girl*," the traveler scoffed. "A *girl* is going to give me some relief? You're not a pimp trying to sell me some tired old hooker, are you?"

"Hey, no way, Ace." The apostle Simon who wanted to be called Peter told him. "This chick is a-number-one genuine, the real article!" and adding a wink, "She's the savior the Rabbis say God sent to guide the people of Israel!"

"Well, I don't know," the cat laid on them, "a girl savior?"

"Give me some skin, Jackson," Jessica smiled, approaching the crippled man with her right hand extended.

"This isn't going to cost me anything?" the man asked suspiciously, holding his own hand back from her as though she might try to steal his watch.

"No, baby," Jessica replied. Then turning to her flock of followers, she shouted, "Has someone got one of those portable massage tables?

Jessica's friends helped the cat with the bent frame up onto the makeshift board and stretched him out, face down. Jessica approached the table, cracking her knuckles. She laid her hands on the man's back, walking a light touch of fingers along the cat's spine.

"Wow," she said. "Man your lumbar is way out of line. And your sciatic discs are pretty bad too!" She leaned all her weight into the man's back, which gave forth with a loud crack or two.

"Now roll over," she told the man. "I need to check your neck as well!"

Jessica placed her slender fingers against the man's jaw, twisting his neck left and right which brought out a few more loud clicks. Then she stepped back.

"Get up and walk!" she commanded. The man moved his head left to look at her, with a face that said she was crazy, but then he broke into a smile.

"So now it doesn't hurt to move my neck!" he speculated.

"It shouldn't anymore, now that your top cervical disc has broken free…"

"Listen, girlie, I don't know from this cervical, lumbar and whatever…"

"Just get up from the table," Jessica commanded him.

The man extended a hesitant right leg, rolled over and when he felt no pain, he wiggled around and stood… then he reached his hands skyward and stretched as the smile on his face grew ever wider.

"Miracle!" came the murmur from the crowd, then louder, "Miracle! It's a miracle!"

God's voice spoke softly in Jessica's ear. "Don't you dare say the word chiropractic! It's our little secret for at least another eighteen hundred years. Then God smiled. "Miracle! I like the sound of that! We'll have to work out a few more of these."

XI

Jessica mulled this miracle thing over in her head for a bit. "I definitely have a talent along these lines," she told herself. "I better keep my eyes peeled for some more opportunities to do these kinds of acts."

On the highway outside Haifa that afternoon, Jessica and her merry men came upon two young blind guys helping each other to slowly make their way.

"Where are you men headed?" she asked the pair.

"We are headed to the temple in the city to pray," responded the taller of the two lads.

"We lost our sight some years ago," added his brother, "and we go almost daily to pray for our poor departed mother, and that someday we may see again."

"How did you come to be blinded?" Luke asked.

"It is an old story," the first man replied. "Are you sure you want to hear?"

"Of course we do," assured James in a kind voice. "Every man's suffering is our suffering as well. Your tale is important to us."

"Well," the shorter of the two replied hesitantly. "It was at Hanukkah, many years ago. In that year, Hanukkah fell very close to the Roman Saturnalia and many Romans were also celebrating in our village. As a prank, one of the soldiers snuck a Roman candle into our **Menorah, but we knew nothing of his little** joke.

"My brother and I were standing close by when our mother lit the candle. Mother was hit by the rocket and died. My brother and I were blinded by the flash of flame."

"That is a horrible story," Judas said. "And were these soldiers punished?"

"Alas, we are but poor Hebrew people," the taller brother answered. "We are not at all valued by the rulers of the Roman world."

Jessica turned and winked at her disciples. "Show time," she whispered. "I may need a chorus here, so watch me for queues."

"It is a shame you lost your sight," Jessica taunted them, "because if you could see me, you'd be looking at the hottest little mama on the planet!"

Taking their cue, the disciples sang out in a cappella, "Amen!"

Confusion contorted the two unseeing faces. What was this woman trying to say to them?

"You ever hear the expression 'she could give eyesight to the blind?'" Jessica asked them. "Some sweet and hot bodied woman that looked just too good to miss? Well that's me! I'm reet, petite and oh so neat! My name is Jessica Crystal and some say I'm the one that's come to save all the children of Israel!"

The chorus gave out with hoots and cat calls.

"And I'm not wearing anything under my robe!" she taunted.

The two blind men started to sweat.

"So now, right here on this spot, I want you to pray. Pray harder than you ever have before in your young lives. You say those prayers, and Mother God will be listening as I throw off my robe!"

The pair fell to their knees, the sweat pouring off of them and their lips moving rapidly. And then, the shorter of the two jumped up, but he didn't look directly in Jessica's direction at first. His peepers rolled heavenward, then swept down across the landscape, finally coming to rest on Jessica's face. And as his eyes traveled over her still robed figure he fell to his knees once more and bowed his head.

About that time, the brother's eyes opened, focused directly on Jessica's chest, but quickly traveled up to her face. The word "miracle" formed on his lips and he clasped his hands before him in prayer.

"There's that miracle thing again," Jessica winked at her twelve compadres. "I like the sound of that word!"

"Eyesight to the blind," the shorter of the former blind men laughed. "You have quite a sense of humor for a savior. And I don't know how we can thank you enough! We are the luckiest men alive!"

Mother God appeared on low beam, low enough that only Jessica could see her. "Inciting a bit of lust? Is that the way you were taught to do things?"

"Hey, it worked, Mother God. What can I say?"

"Who am I to argue with success?" God asked. "But I still think you'd better go back and read through your Torah again, capisce?"

XII

"So listen," God told Jessica a week or so later, "I've been thinkin' about this miracle thing. There's a troop of lepers coming to town, so I've got you booked into Morrie's Mashuga Shack. You know, that little comedy improve club in the town center?"

"What am I supposed to do at the Mashuga Shack?" Jessica asked with a skeptical look.

"Well, you know, maybe a little stand-up comedy for the lepers, tell a few jokes, get a few laughs!"

"Huh?" Jessica took a step backwards in confusion.

"Hey, laughter is the best medicine!" God cackled. "And remember, I said that first 'cause somewhere down the line some playwright or other is gonna try and claim it for their own."

Jessica wasn't sure what to think, but God was God, so she went home and tried to put together a little routine she could deliver at the club. Lepers? Rotting flesh? What could be funny about that? 'Can Johnny come out and play? Johnny has leprosy. Can we come in and watch him rot?' Oh, Mother God, what are you asking of me?

When open mic night came around and the lepers filed into the club, Jesse still had some butterflies in her stomach. After all, she wasn't really a comedienne. She was a carpenter and part time preacher, or so they said.

The room was about half full when Jessica took the stage. The lepers were grouped on one side of the aisle, the regulars packed against the wall on the other side, leaning away from the diseased half of the audience.

Jessica fought down her stage fright. "So did you hear about the leper colony prize fight? It was a real face-off."

Jessica's opening joke was met with a dead silence, but soon from the rear of the crowd came a small titter. Then everyone was laughing loud and hard. Jesse told another poor taste leper joke, then another. The laughter grew until a voice rang out, "Hey, what the fah? I'm healed! I'm whole!"

Soon others were making their sounds of comfort and amazement and the word "miracle" could be heard rippling through both sides of the crowd.

God briefly materialized on low beam, gave Jessica a stage wink with a thumbs-up and shimmered out.

The rest of Jessica's prepared routine was largely lost behind shouts of disbelief and cries of "miracle." At the end of her performance, most of the cured lepers filed out, slapping each other on the back and talking about Jessica's wonderful performance. Only one leper came up to the stage and thanked her!

The headlines of the next morning's Nazareth Nabob Reporter sang the praises of this young Jewish girl who cured a whole busload of lepers with a handful of old bad jokes!

XIII

With her success as a stand-up comic, Jessica decided to take a little time off for the holidays. She decided to head home to Nazareth for Passover even though God said it was no big thing.

"All this lamb's blood, it's just gross!" God told her. "Why should innocent lambs die when people celebrate? I blame that Ibrahim guy again! Why can't people just listen?"

Jessica shrugged her shoulders. What did she know about Ibrahim? I mean outside what she read in the Torah.

"So what I want you to do," God told her with a wistful look, "I want you to stage a little civil disobedience at the temple here.

"We've got a lot of business wankers trying to profit off the temple. These guys are offering to loan money, already! And they're selling sacrificial animals; oxen, doves, pigeons and such! Animals that you and I know are sacred, just like all my living creatures!"

"So what should I do, Mother God?" Jessica asked.

"Be creative!" came her reply. "You're a creative girl. You'll think of something!"

From behind her, Jessica heard Simon, the one who wasn't known as Peter, complaining to one of the locals about how the municipality's dog catcher was far too ready to kill the strays they picked up in the streets of Nazareth.

Turning, she called to him. "They have too many stray dogs?"

Skoot Larson

"Whippets," came Peter's reply. "Somebody has turned loose a plague of whippets."

Jessica gave a knowing nod. "Whippets are just what we need," she told him. "Go forth and rescue the lot of them. We'll put these mini-greyhounds to work, save their lives and do Mother God a favor as well."

"With a bunch of anorexic puppies? the other Peter's brother, Andrew, mused.

"God works in mysterious ways," Jessica replied, "and so do I!"

And so the double gross of skinny dogs were rounded up and herded into the temple. Their yapping quickly drowned out the sound of businessmen hawking their wares, while the rambunctious canines knocked over displays and threaded themselves between the legs of potential customers. The money changers and sellers of sacrificial animals were quick to raise their voices in complaint, but they couldn't be heard over the pack of baying hounds.

Jessica walked among them, telling them that this was her Mother's house. Mother God did not appreciate their presence in *her* establishment. She shouted to them over and over that they were not welcome here, and, in fact, were not really welcome anywhere in the Hebrew realm. They were, in fact, turning God's Temple into a den of inequity through their commercial activities.

"Then what are we to do? This is our livelihood." asked one of the biggest business owners.

"No concern of mine," Jessica told him, "How about you rent some space on the poor side of town. You can hang three balls outside your door and loan money against people's possessions,

- 52 -

like carpenter tools, holy day suits and domestic animals? God probably won't approve, but at least you'll be out of the temple. And you'll still be working."

"You think we could do this?" asked one of the men.

"Why don't you ask the folks at the Better Business Bureau," Jessica told him.

"I think we'll try it without asking anyone else's opinion," the man told her, "Once bitten, twice shy."

XIV

As the people around Nazareth heard the rumors of this Jewish girl who performed miracles, there was a lot of speculation about what she was trying to accomplish. Some said she was collecting a whole bunch of souls in a net that she would later review and cast the bad ones out. Or that she was like a farmer dude that found a great treasure on some land, sold the treasure and used his gains to purchase the land. Or someone finding a really cool and valuable pearl and spending all his rent money to possess the thing.

These are parables, Jessica told her inner circle. People seem to dig parables, so maybe we should offer some up for them.

And pondering this, Jessica went outside and walked down to the beach. She sat down in a little dingy with a red sail to think things over and soon a crowd of folks started gathering on the sand in front of her.

"Talk to us, oh wise chick," a tall bearded man shouted from the shoreline. Jessica decided to give this parable wheeze a go.

"Behold," she loudly proclaimed, "a sower went out to sow."

"Oh wise seer, tell us more," a short, balding dude in the front row barked.

"As he sowed," Jessica continued, ignoring the interruptions, "some of the seeds fell into the wind, landing all around. Clever small birds hopped out and devoured many of these stray seeds, dig? And some other seeds fell on the rocks that didn't hold much soil to give them roots. When the hot sun came out, these babies got scorched and didn't stand a chance.

"And some fell into bushes with thorns, and when they tried to do their thing, the thorns choked these little suckers out!"

"Wow, solid downer," lamented a hippie-looking chick in tie-dyed robes with a couple small babies.

"Hey, but it's cool," Jessica continued. "'Cause lots of these little seed gems fell into good earth as bird poop where they yielded tons of really tasty fruit for all the cats and kitties to scarf down. Can you dig it?"

"Yeah baby, we can dig it!" came the loud reply.

"So, what's with the riddler bit," Thad inquired, the other disciples nodding their heads behind him.

Jessica smiled, "These people are simple folks. We lay it on them in these parables and wise sayings and they're much more likely to cop to what we're putting down here. It's a long story, you know? If we start rappin' about sowing souls for heaven, it might go over their heads, but when we lay it down light, tight and right in a little fairy story, then move on from there, little light bulbs can go off in their heads."

She laid another story on the crowd about some chick hiding yeast in her bread and the bread rising, but some of the young men in the crowd starting asking why she didn't use the yeast to make something cool like beer.

Ignoring the youths, Jessica went on to put it down that these seeds and yeast and all were like folks knockin' on heaven's door. "Can you all dig it? she shouted.

"Right on, sister," came their strong reply. "We got it!"

XV

Later, Jessica tried to take her act to her own synagogue where she found a really tough audience to try and reach. "Where did this local girl get all these wild ideas and these crazy powers?" the neighborhood rabble wanted to know. "I think this babe is getting' way above her raisin'!"

"Just a simple carpenter's daughter," one woman tsked. "Ain't this the girl child of that crazy Mary woman? The sister to these twelve boys that just hang around talking and never seem to do a lick of honest work?"

"I think we better blow this Popsicle stand," Jessica whispered to her little troop. To the crowd, she announced, "A prophet is not without honor except in his own environs!"

And Jessica left without giving them any of the miracles they were likely to just scoff at anyway.

About this same time, the son of old King Harry started getting the news about Jessica, the savior chick that had eluded his dumb dad because the senior Harry had just assumed a savior had to be a man. "Maybe it's this crazy Baptist fellow, like raised from the dead with all this magic shit running through him."

Harry had earlier snared Baptist John and locked him away in a cell, but, much as he wanted to waste the man, he was afraid he might lose some market share with his loyal subjects that held this man to be a prophet.

Harry was holding John on charges of mouthing off about some very deserving and privileged upper class folks being adulterers! Big deal! Didn't rank have its special perks?

Mother God was really drug when she heard that King Harry had lopped the head off Crazy John the B. Some of Jessica's disciple cats were there for the dinner when this loony girlfriend of King Harry came waltzing in with John's lifeless head on a silver platter.

Jessica's guys were so upset that they couldn't stay for the main course of the meal. They made their exit and headed back to their boat, with what they'd already consumed rising in their throats, threatening to come up all over their tunics.

They sailed down the coast as they recovered from the gross sight of poor John's bloodied head, and returned to shore a few miles away where they found a hungry crowd. Jessica was there and healed a few of the ones who were feeling less than fit, but the crowds just wouldn't disperse.

Her fellows grumbled that they should "just go home and grab a TV dinner or something," but Jessica was cool.

"Let's give them a little grub," she told her disciples. "We can surely spare something."

Thad spoke up to say, "We've only got, like five loaves of challah and a couple small fish."

Jessica asked that they pass the dwindling food stuffs to her. She took the basket and gave a wink heavenward to Mother God before handing out food stuffs to the crowd. To everyone's amazement, the more bits of bread Jessica broke off to give away, the more seemed to appear in her basket, and much the same with the fish's fillets.

In the end, some five thousand men, women and children were served Jessica's little Happy Meals! It proved a banner day for the Daughter of God's little ministry, although there were still doubters in the Synagogue.

XVI

While Jessica fulfilled all her duties for Mother God in a timely manner, she kept after the woman about the travels she longed to make to other lands, where she might learn about cultures beyond her own. In her mind, Jessica romanticized about the Irish folks with their music and dancing. She was also curious about the warlike tribes in the cold climes of the farthest north, as well as the mystics of the Orient and the Far East. In dreams, she also saw peaceful natives far across the oceans that lived in harmony with nature in the land around them.

Jessica now had twelve well-trained disciples who aided her in her ministries. She believed in each of them and trusted that they could do her work while she took a long sabbatical to increase her own knowledge and experience.

Mother God smiled down, knowing that everything in the area around Nazareth was under control. She went over all the facts in her head and decided it was time to grant the young savior her fervent request.

Shortly before dawn, Mother God shimmered down on low beam, so as not to wake up the whole neighborhood. "Jesse girl? You awake?" A coffee colored hand shook Jessica's shoulder and the girl's eyes popped open, fully awake.

"Mother God, you startled me!"

"Sorry girl," the great Lady apologized. "But listen, this little bit of traveling you've been asking me about? I think it might be time!"

Jessica's face burst into a broad grin and she clapped her hands together. "Oh thank you, Mother God! Where do I begin... and *how*?"

"I think we should make the far north your first stop. Spend some time with the Viking people and from there we'll plan a path to the south and east, how's that sound?"

"Viking people? You know best, Mother God... but how will I get there? Am I going to have to walk all that way?"

Suddenly, before her very eyes, God morphed into a tall man with bright copper hair and beard. She had only one eye, the other's socket simply a dark hole.

Jessica drew a sharp intake of breath. "Mother God?" she asked in a slightly fearful voice.

"Of course it's me, sweetie!" came the voice Jessica knew to be God's. "But where you're going, they see me as a very wise old man. They all call me Odin! They believe I know and see all because I have a pair of ravens that fly around the world bringing me all the news, and that I have a pair of wolves that protect me from harm. Their legend says that I gave my eye in trade for all the wisdom in the universe."

"Is this true?" Jessica asked in wonderment.

"Trading the eye, no, but the rest of it? It is to them, sweetie. Also, I have a circle of twelve helpers there, kinda like your disciples, you know? That magic number twelve," she chuckled. "The people there think of them as being Gods just like me, and who am I to spoil their little party?

"You'll get to meet them all soon."

Outside her bedroom window, Jessica heard a horse whinny. "That'll be your ride." Mother God gave her a wink.

Jesse went to the window and peered out into dawn's first light. Outside her house stood a tall gray stallion at least seven hands high... and the horse appeared to be standing on *eight legs*! How could this be?

Mother God saw the look on her face and laughed. "Don't worry, sweetie. This is my, or rather Odin's horse. I call him Sleipnir and, yes, he does have eight legs. He can practically fly, which is how we're going to get you over the mountains beyond Rome and up to the frozen north.

"But first, you'll need to let your buddies know that you're off on a little mission and they may not see you around for a year or so. I'll just keep Sleipnir under wraps here with me until around midnight tonight. Pack what you'll need for the journey and when everyone's asleep, I'll come back and tap on your window."

XVII

All her disciples were very curious as to where Jessica was going, and why. She felt that she shouldn't tell them too much. It would be better to surprise them with all she might learn when she returned to Nazareth. Why put their expectations too high when she, herself, wasn't all that sure of what might await her. Only Mother God knew where it would all lead, and she wasn't saying all that much about it beyond that she felt Jessica was ready.

"See that my ministry goes on, as it has," Jessica told them, uncorking a clay bottle of good red. "That's all I ask of you," she told them. "I only hope that I'll have more to share when I return. I just know I'll be better equipped to minister to our people when I've learned what there is to know about the world beyond the Roman occupied states. So be it!"

The disciples nodded like a circle of bobble-head dolls. "We'll just keep fishing for souls," Johnny told her with wide eyes as he sipped from his cup.

"You got it, guys," Jessica told them with a wink. "I know you can handle it."

Matthew asked if Jesse needed anything for her journey, to which Jessica replied, "God will provide."

Andrew came forward with a sack of dried fish anyway. "Just in case you get hungry on your trip," he told her. "I know you won't always be walking at the seaside and you'll probably miss your fish."

Jessica took his right hand in both of hers and thanked Andrew profusely. "You are all so thoughtful and caring," she told them. "That's how I know I can trust you to do God's work in my absence."

They drank wine until late in the evening, when all the disciples seemed to nod off at once. Jessica was a bit mystified as she barely had a buzz on herself, but then Mother God shimmered up to the window.

"Time to saddle up, Jesse girl," she whispered, so as not to awaken the twelve men. "We've got a nice clear night, not too cold, so let's take off."

Jessica mounted the eight-legged horse behind Mother God. Sleipnir pawed the ground for a beat or two, then threw his head back and leaped toward the sky. Eight legs pumping, they were soon flying over the desert sands, Nazareth rapidly disappearing in their rear view mirror.

The powerful beast soared over the Greek Isles and Rome itself. Lake Como came into view and then went along with the Matterhorn. With the Alpine mountains far below, Sleipnir's eight legs kept pumping. They passed over green river valleys, then a large body of water, finally touching down in a deep fjord cut into a tall west-facing mountain side.

XVIII

As they landed, a large group of hairy men holding shields over their bodies and heavy hammers in their hands stepped forward to meet them. When they recognized Sleipnir, they lowered their shields and came forward to greet Mother God and Jessica. As Jessica dismounted, she could see that Mother God was once again the tall one-eyed, red headed man she'd met earlier in Nazareth.

Jessica dismounted and stood in front of the warriors. The men knelt before her, heads down and silent. Mother God, in the guise of Odin, introduced Jessica as another God, one who dwelt in the warm lands to the south, waiting to welcome those Vikings who might someday venture so far from home.

The Viking warriors quickly invited Jessica to follow them to their village, where she could meet their wives and children. Jessica followed gladly, walking rather than riding on the back of Sleipnir.

The children were the first to approach her. One of the young boys was lame, with a withered leg. Jessica summoned power from Mother God, and healed the lad on the spot.

Within moments, all the women were surrounding her and praising her actions. Mother God Odin appeared briefly overhead to wink her one eye at Jessica.

The Viking people brought Jessica into a long building fashioned from pine logs and mud. They all sat around a table that was also made of pine. One of the women passed around vessels that had been fashioned from the horns of bulls. A second lady followed with an enormous pewter flagon, filling the horn mugs with strong, dark ale.

One small sip of the honey and malt beverage sent Jesse's head reeling, but she told herself that she could handle the alcohol, knowing Mother God wouldn't allow her to fail.

A tall, brown-haired man at the head of the table announced that his men had recently slain a small herd of reindeer, so they would be having a feast as soon as the meat had been properly seasoned and cooked.

The other men at the table drank lots of ale and talked about fishing. Although they consumed horn after horn of the potent drink, no one appeared to be affected by it.

Then a young man in his teens thought to ask Jessica what she was God of. Never having thought of herself as a God, Jessica stumbled over her words in search of a credible answer. After a few false starts, she finally blurted out, "I am the God of Peace!"

Conversations around the table stopped as all the assembled guests looked around at her.

"I pray for you, that someday *you'll* find peace and not fear your neighbors," Jessica told them.

A tall Blond Viking rose from his seat. "We fear nothing, Lady Peace God," he told her. "But rather, we live in a land with very little good earth to farm, only small plots to feed our people. We have little to leave to our children except the ability to fight and conquer other lands where we may someday grow the crops they need!"

Jessica was perplexed. She looked over her shoulder for some sign from Mother God, but Mother God was nowhere to be seen. And then there came a loud pounding on the stout oak door to the hall.

XIX

The brown haired captain at the head of the table shouted, "Enter," and a mixed group of folks filed in standing behind vacant seats at the lower end of the table. They were twelve in number with Odin, the thirteenth, bringing up the rear and pulling the door closed behind them.

"We are entertaining Jessica, the God of Peace from some distant land to the south," Odin announced to his troop. "Jessica, may I present my son Thor, the God of Love and War…"

An amazing hulk of a man, also red-headed and bearded, took a step forward and nodded his head in greeting to Jessica.

"And this," Odin continued, "is my wife, Frigg, God of the Family and Earth Mother. And on my other side we have Freyr. She is the God of Plenty, to see that we have abundance in our crops, our fishing and our hunting."

The two ladies by Odin's side wore long blond braids falling almost to their waists, and they curtsied to Jessica.

"And we have Baldur the Good…" A very handsome white-haired man dressed in a sparkling white polar bear skin bowed his head to Jessica.

"Baldur is probably the closest thing we have here to a God of Peace." Jessica smiled at this latest God who she assumed was, like her, a force for good.

Just then a small dark man standing behind Odin passed a loud blast of gas that sounded like the pedal tone of a bass trombone. The other's looked away in embarrassment. "And this would be Loki, the God of Mischief," Odin intoned with a frown. Loki glanced in Jessica's direction but offered neither a greeting nor an apology.

A tall and angry lady with fiery red hair stepped from behind Loki, waving her hand in front of her face with a scowl. "And this would be Freyja, God of Anger and Unrest," Odin chuckled.

"You actually have such a God? Someone to bring unrest and anger?" Jessica asked.

"More to help us deal with these things," Thor rumbled.

Next a thin man with a sort of harp stepped smiling from behind Freyja and Loki.

"And Bragi they call me, don't know why,

I'm just a rhyming kind of guy

I speak in verse, just as I write

Sagas I tell when we win a fight

And if that's not enough to make you smile

Then with song and dance I'll your heart beguile…"

And with that he started to strum a lovely tune.

"Ah yes," Odin grinned, our God of Poetry and Music always likes to introduce himself!"

Jessica was soon lost trying to remember who was God of what as she met the others; Tyr, the God of Justice; Sif, God of Fertility; Idunn, God of Youth and Nanna, of Joy. They all seemed to blend together. Jessica was glad that her old Torah teachings were not this complicated apart from all that who was begetting who.

The drinking and feasting went on until late in the night. Jessica, feeling a bit jet-lagged from her long flight across the European continent, was fading fast. Mother God, in her Odin persona, noticed the effect the long party and strong drink was having on Jessica and raised a toast to peace, suggesting after the ale had gone down that their guest should be given a pallet in the lodge where she could rest from her long journey. The toast turned into three or four more; to her, to Sleipnir and finally all the Gods drained their horns in a salute to themselves. Then a bed was prepared and Jessica stumbled off to a troubled sleep, dreaming of battles with hammers smashing flesh and the slaughter of friendly creatures.

XX

The next morning, she was awakened by Odin's wife, Frigg, speaking in the voice of Mother God. "Jesse? Listen, we've got a big day ahead of us. I think you should rise and shine. You'll have to bathe in the fjord, but it's not as cold as it looks."

"Frigg?" Jessica mouthed. "But you sound like Mother God."

"Of course I do, sweetie," came the reply. "I'm all of these Gods, in case you hadn't notice. Oy, I know what it's like to be a split personality, believe me!" She dramatically raised one wrist up to her brow, then smiled. "What? You think I'd trust some kind of heathen strangers?" God laughed loudly at her little joke. "Come on, already! I am the eggplant and I am the walrus, coo coo ca choo… No, wait a minute, that's not from your time either…."

Jessica looked at her with confused eyes. "Somewhere along the line, I really should hip you to these guys called the Beatles, Mother God laid on her. But that's another story." And Mother God faded away.

Jessica walked out into brilliant sunshine, but the temperature was frigid. How could it be so cold with the sun shining as bright as this?

The Viking people didn't seem to notice the chilly air. Sailors mended nets on the docks wearing only short pants and singlets, as their women carried clothes to the beach to be washed in the salty water of the fjord. Other shirtless men pushed rope caulking between planks on the side of a long boat. Children roamed the docks and the village green, kicking balls around the grassy areas by the dockside and throwing sticks for the village dogs to fetch. No one appeared hung over from the previous day's feasting. The village hummed with energy.

Jessica smiled at the strength and resilience of these northern people. They certainly knew how to live life! They seemed so much more up-beat and positive then the Hebrew people of her home-land who were always burdened down with guilt about one thing or another. But, on the other hand, they lived by the sword and the hammer. How could they find peace in the world living surround-ed by such violence, so close to death?

Jessica was stepping onto a wide pier that extended out into the fjord when she noticed a group of small boys climbing the ropes to one of the village's long boats. The boat was loosely tied and no one stood watch on her deck.

As the boys shinnied up the hawser, a large rat started down from the boat's main deck. The young fellows on the pier shouted out that the rat would bite their friends and they would die, with no chance of ever achieving Valhalla, which was reserved for warriors who died in battle against other *men*, not small rodents. Fighting a small creature didn't qualify as dying in battle!

The boy highest up the rope tried to back down, but was met by the resistance of the lads behind him. In a panic, he let go of the line and dropped into the chilly waters of the fjord, where he proceeded to flounder about, momentarily forgetting how to swim.

Without thinking, Jessica went into her 'Savior' mode. She took a hesitant step, then another from the quayside along the fjord. Feeling Mother God behind her, Jessica easily put one foot in front of the other, stepping lightly over the waters without sinking to rescue the young boy. She was once again walking on water!

She hardly realized what she was doing, but the ladies of the village standing on the quayside quickly clocked her miracle. Jessica walked atop the light harbor chop until she reached the boy, whom she grabbed by the scruff of his neck and dragged him back to shore.

When the boy was returned to the arms of his parents, another feast was proclaimed. Jessica was carried on the shoulders of stout Viking men back to the common hall, where more strong ale was served up and an amazing table of fresh cod fish was laid out.

Bragi recited a poem about this God who could walk atop the fjord's chilly surface, his words taunting the other Gods to try such a feat. Thor swore that he could do this, and he would show them all, but when they goaded him on to "do it now," he said he didn't want to be a showoff and make the guest Lady God embarrassed about the simplicity of her miracle.

How could she capitalize on these events to further her ministry? Jessica was at a loss. These folks were happy with their lives and had their own strong beliefs, miracles being a part of their faith. She tried to summon Mother God, but got no response. After her restless night and the events of the morning, Jessica decided she'd had enough of the far north tribe and longed for God to take her south, to the Celtic people who danced and played bagpipes! Surely they would not be as weird as these Viking folks with their wars and constant drinking!

Jessica endured another couple hours in the long lodge with this loud, happy tribe of fair skinned people. When the plates held only the bones of the barbequed fish and the latest keg of ale ran dry, the men and women alike filed outside to resume the tasks they had been working at and Jessica got her long awaited bath.

In the small secluded cove where Jessica had entered the water, she emerged to find Mother God looking just like her normal self, at least to Jesse, holding out a linen towel to her.

"So I got your message," God chuckled. "You're not much of a party girl but you think you're ready for the next party" God laughed out loud at this, shaking her head.

"How about after you thank these folks for their hospitality and say your farewells, we girls take a little trip up the mountain. I know a quiet place you can get a good night's sleep before the next party begins."

"Oh, Mother God, must I stay here for another party?"

"Not *here*, Jesse girl," Mother God tutted. "I mean the party in Galway! You think these northerners can drink? Wait'll you catch the Irish!"

Returning to the lodge from her bath, Jessica announced to the Viking village that she had been summoned home in an emergency. Although she truly wanted to stay and party with the North men, her own people were desperately in need of her guidance and she had to go back at once.

The Viking people understood, each in turn coming forth to give her a hug and express their pleasure in meeting such an intriguing God.

XXI

Mother God found Jessica a stout and straight tree branch that she could use as a walking stick and led her to a path by the shoreline of the fjord.

It was easy going at first, then the path grew narrow and steep with many switchbacks. They kept climbing up the mountain for the better part of the afternoon. By the time the trail began to level off, the sun was almost touching the sea on the horizon. They crossed a grassy meadow where a few sheep wandered, then climbed for another stretch to a level grove of evergreen trees. In the center of the stand of conifers they came upon a deep pile of pine needles and birch leaves.

Jessica threw herself down and rolled about in the soft bed. With a big grin she said, "Thank you, Mother God."

God knelt down and kissed Jessica's forehead. "I'll see you in the morning, kid," she winked. "I gotta head back down the mountain so I don't miss tonight's party. I hear Bragi has written some long, cool verse about you, my dear! It sounds like these people will remember you for a long time."

Jessica was asleep even before God's light shimmered out of view. Her sleep was deep and dreamless. She awoke in what seemed to her only an instant to the sound of bird song. The bright sun was already clearing the high mountain top above her. She sat up to find the bushes around her were heavy with small juicy red berries. She picked a handful to eat, sharing them with the birds that periodically landed on the bushes.

Jessica emerged from her little copse to search for the stream she heard in the distance. She was washing the berry juice from around her lips when Mother God materialized just over the nearby cliff. Sleipnir hovered in the air by her side.

"All rested and ready for some more travel? It should be a good day for flying." God landed by her side. "Let me tell you, hon, you made quite an impression back at the fjord! Bragi even wrote an epic about why not give peace a chance."

"Oh, God… do you think they might?"

"Sure, maybe for a week or three… until the next guy gets angry over losing a game of dice or some stranger wanders into the area they claim as their hunting ground."

"Oh, but Mother God."

"Relax kid, you didn't come here to preach, you came here to learn about the world, and you still got *a lot* to learn! Listen, by the time we get to the library in Alexandria, you are going to be one smart cookie!"

"Alexandria, like in Egypt?" Jessica asked.

"That's the place. Bet you didn't even know it was there. But hey, right now it's time for your long awaited trip to Galway, and it ain't nothing like Galilee, believe me on this!"

Jessica climbed onto Sleipnir's broad back. The animal's eight hooves thundered across the meadow, over the cliff and they were once again airborne.

XXII

The Emerald Isle was lush, green and beautiful in the afternoon sun as Sleipnir coasted down the off-shore breeze toward the northwest coast. They landed on a secluded stretch of sand at the edge of the island's vast forest. Sleipnir turned pale and sort of faded into thin air when Jessica had dismounted. As Jessica turned, Mother God had been replaced by a character that would have taken Jessica to the Haight-Ashbury neighborhood of 1960's San Francisco if she'd known about such a place in time; God had turned into a beatifically beaming Hippie.

This Celtic Earth Mother put an arm around Jessica's shoulder and pulled her close for a snug hug. She was a stately woman with bright red hair and piercing blue eyes. God looked like a happier version of Freyja, the Viking God of Anger. The Earth Mother wore soft leather leggings under a flowing skirt that was tie-dyed with the juices of beet root, saffron, green grass and something dark blue that Jessica didn't recognize.

"The tribe awaits us back in the village," said the old voice of God that she recognized, with just a hint of extra huskiness to it.

Where Sleipnir had stood moments before a small white pony with a long mane and a horn on its forehead shimmered into existence. A unicorn? No, that couldn't be. The unicorn was a mystical beast!

The Earth Mother shrugged her shoulders. "Hey, I'm God. I can create *any* kind animal I want to!" She patted Jessica's shoulder, then swept her other hand out to indicate a path into the trees. The unicorn was already headed toward the trail.

They hadn't walked far when Jessica heard the music of harps, tin whistles and, yes, bagpipes in the distance. She clasped her hands together before her chest, almost in a motion of prayer. "Oh, thank you, Mother God. Oh, that music is heavenly!" God turned to her and winked.

Following the joyful strains of song, they soon arrived at a clearing filled with more hippie type folks. While a small group at the center played the various instruments Jessica recognized from her early dreams, others sat in the grass clapping hands, or gleefully danced around the wide meadow.

The merry crowd tipped their cloth caps or nodded their heads to Jessica in welcome. From a small cabin at the clearing's edge, a heavy-set girl with almost black hair came forward and handed Jessica a tall clay jug, motioning that she was to drink from it.

The ale in the earthenware vessel tasted a little sweeter than what the Vikings had offered, but she could tell that the drink was just as potent. She cast a glance at Earth Mother God, but God just shrugged her shoulders as she began moving her leather-clad feet to the syncopated rhythm.

After a few more swallows of the Irish ale, Jessica's feet started moving with the gay tune as well. From the jig they'd been performing, the musicians modulated into a fast reel and many of the dancers joined hands to form a giant circle around the players of music. The children of the village darted between the dancer's legs and formed their own small circle between the adults and the band. A man holding a fiddle down along his chest broke through the moving people to add his own sound to the ensemble, and when he had established himself as one of them, he pushed the pace of their reel faster and faster until Jessica was having a hard time lifting her feet quickly enough to keep up with the others.

Sweat poured off dancers and musicians alike as the circle moved around the meadow in a fast trot. Then one of the folks tripped over his own feet and the merry makers behind him fell over the man as well and everyone broke into gales of happy laughter.

The music slowed once more and then stopped, leaving only the dying drone from the pipes which still contain a breath of the piper's air within them.

Still laughing, the village inhabitants began to rise up from the grass. A few stayed down, kissing playfully and holding hands. God placed herself center stage, in front of the exhausted musicians.

"Me lairds and m'ladies," she called out to them. "We have a guest in our midst. Welcome her! Her name is Jessica, and she is an Earth Mother like myself, but from the lands far across the channel, beyond that coast where the primitives dwell."

"Primitives?" Jessica wondered. "Who were the primitives? Maybe some people God intended to introduce her to later? Or could it be those violent Viking people?"

The Irish folks all rushed up, each in turn greeting her warmly and hugging her. One little girl of about six years brought Jessica a necklace fashioned from seashells and some kind of large nuts. Were they chestnuts? An older man with a wreath of leaves in his hair knelt on one knee and kissed her hand.

"I am Liam," he announced, "the leading tribal elder. We are always glad to have visitors from distant lands, as long as they come in peace. You do come in peace, do you not?"

"Of course she comes in peace," Earth Mother God laughed. "I guided her here to you! I, who bring you good harvests and good hunting."

The man bowed his head in Mother God's direction. "Of course, Earth Mother," he spoke in a low, humble tone. "The Chief Druid has mentioned that you might bring such a guest. I apologize for my doubting."

"You're alright, Liam." God told him. "You can get up now. Listen, I think our guest's flagon is running low. Why don't you bring the small keg and refill her ale, then when the players have rested, we'll have more music and dance!"

XXIII

When the sun hung low in the sky, Liam called them all to a wide and long table behind the small grouping of huts and outbuildings. Places were set along its length and the table's center held platters of roasted game birds. More kegs of the sweet ale that they told Jessica was called Mead were stacked close to the feasting board. Liam requested that Jessica sit to his left at the head of the table. Mother God took the stool to his right.

Diners filled their earthenware mugs on the way to their seats. A boy in his teens was stationed near the rack of kegs to see that no one's drink ran low once they were seated. Another young man with a long wooden fork circled the guests spearing the cooked hens and delivering them to the plates of the villagers. There was a low mumble of conversation throughout the crowd as the mead oiled their tongues.

When each of the villagers had a bird, some greens and a few mushrooms on their plate, Liam raised his hand to give a sign and they all dug into their meal.

Conversation lulled as the revelers demolished the feast set before them. When the last scrap had been chewed and swallowed, Liam stood and spoke in a loud voice.

"A toast to our lovely visitor!" And he raised his own jug high. "The Gods be with you," the crowd shouted in unison.

"And what can you tell us about the people in your land?" a lady a few stools down from Jessica asked her. "Is it green as our <u>Érenn</u>? And do you have such tasty game hens as we are blessed with?"

Jessica wiped juice from her lips on a linen napkin. "We are primarily fishermen. We bake bread and eat the bounty the sea brings us. Our land is not so green as your <u>Érenn</u>." She thought for a minute. Would these people know what a sandy desert was? She went on to try and explain.

"The land I dwell in is sandy, like your little beach, and the air is always hot and dry."

There were sounds of surprise and disbelief from around the table.

"And why would your people choose to live in such a place?" Liam asked with true curiosity.

"It is all we know," Jessica started. "All we have ever known! But we are happy there. We have our temples and our families..."

"*I* would never live in such a place," snorted the woman from down the table.

"You will be respectful of our guest!" Liam thundered, staring the woman down.

The lady who had misspoken looked down at her empty plate, then contritely held her jug up for a refill.

"My duty is to try and bring peace to my people," Jessica started hesitantly. So far no one had mention war or violence among these Irish people. "You seem to be a very peaceful and loving people."

"We like to think so," Liam replied, wiping the foam from the last sip of drink from his lips with the back of his hand.

"Until someone's had too much drink!" came a rough male voice from down the table. "Then we can all fight with the best of 'em," yelled another.

Jessica broke the uneasy silence that followed. "Please tell me more about your people. Can you share your legends and history?"

Another elder man arose from across the feasting board. He had fading red hair that was going gray around the edges, as was his beard.

"Our Druids tell us we are from the peoples of the Goddess Danu, the <u>Tuatha Dé Danann</u>. It's believed that we have inhabited this island since the world was created." He tipped his head to Mother God, seeming to seek her approval to continue. "Before those of us now here were born, our people faced opposition from many enemies, the most formidable being those led by Balor of the Evil Eye. But he was eventually slain by Lug of the Long Arm at the second battle of Magh Tuireadh. We are protected by the power of the Druids, though they chose to live apart from us. They are our Holy men and give us guidance."

This last statement earned a smirk from God, though she said nothing.

"We bring money to the priests in our temple," Jessica told them. We also use money to buy the goods we need."

Mother God lowered her head slowly moving it back and forth. Maybe Jessica wasn't supposed to talk about money?

"And what is this money?" queried the elder with the graying hair and beard. "I've never heard spoken of anything called money."

And then Jessica realized the can of worms she had opened. "It's a sort of token, uh, brass coins that represent a value so you can buy and sell things, uh…."

"Buy and sell things," repeated a curious Liam. "What sort of things?"

"Well…" Jessica stumbled on. "Say, to buy food, for instance, or to buy mead."

"But we have these things in abundance," roared a voice from the gathered crowd. Our hunters and our brewers supply us according to our needs. We seldom want for anything!"

"Um," Jessica pondered her next words carefully. "We give money to the priests in our temples, so they may serve us undistracted by physical work."

"Priests," harrumphed another man closer to Jessica's seat. "When our Druids are angry or overburdened, we just bring them people that they may sacrifice to whatever God may require it!"

And a silent Jessica, with no good answer to that, thought again about the Vikings with their axes, hammers and shields.

Liam's voice interrupted her thoughts shouting, "Enough of this talk. Where are those musicians and dancers? We should show our guest a good time with song and dance rather than perplex her with our differences!"

XXIV

Drinking and dancing went on until late in the night, long after Jessica began to tire of it. She ended up crawling off to someone's flower bed where she closed her eyes and slept.

In the morning, as Jessica was brushing petals from her hair and wishing she could find a stream to quench the dry mouth left by the previous night's ale, Liam strolled up the path.

"Top of the morning to you, Lady Jessica," he intoned with an impish grin. "And are you enjoying yourself among our humble villagers?"

"Oh yes, of course," Jessica burst forth. "But I do have some questions...."

"Simply ask and I do my best to give satisfaction," Liam grinned.

"I, uh… well… do you people drink and dance all the time?" she blurted out. "How does anything ever get done? Are there slaves or servants that do your bidding?"

Liam laughed. "No slaves here, lassie. We are proud to be free men, the lot of us!"

Jessica rested her chin in her palm to ponder this.

"And we're not lazy," he assured her. "We each of us has our trade, one of the twelve callings."

There was that sacred number twelve again. Jessica's eyes told him to go on.

"We have our healers, hunters, bakers and builders. There are the brewers, the crafters, the teachers and musicians. Then there are weavers, tanners, growers and smiths.

"Magic and wizardry we leave to the Druids. And we elders act as judges and administrators. It's has always been this way and it seems to work well for us."

"And you never have to fight off enemies?" she asked.

"When our people are threatened, every able-bodied man becomes a soldier," the old man proclaimed loudly. "And when there is a disruption of peace among our own, we count on those of us with cooler heads to step up and take control of the situation. Say if two lads start to fight over a game of chance or some bloke raises a hand to strike his wife. We try to be a lawful bunch, but sometimes these things will happen…"

"So it's always a happy and peaceful life for your people!" Jessica replied with a wistful smile.

"Nay, lassie, but it *is* a satisfying life. We take the good along with the bad and live with whatever the world may deliver us. If we dwell on the bad things, it might prevent us from enjoyin' the good." Liam's face was full of contentment as he spoke.

"And I'm thinkin' that you would be looking for the creek where you can wash your face and get a drink to slack your thirst. It would be just down the path behind the feasting table, where the wild blackberries grow." And with that he tipped his cap and started back toward his cottage.

XXV

Earth Mother God was waiting for Jessica beside the small stream of water. "So is this as fantastic as you thought it would be?"

"A little more," Jessica started. "A little much, actually, I mean I love the music and the dancing… Oy, but Roman red wine never gave me such a headache as this! I'm *gesament kaputen!*" She looked up at God and crossed her eyes for effect.

God laughed. "So you want a few more days of this, or are you ready to move on?"

"Can you ask me that in a few hours? Like after I deal with this hangover? I *might* want to spend a little more time here."

God walked with Jessica back to the village, stopping by the flower garden Jessica had crushed the previous night in her slumber, then raised a hand to knock on the door.

In a frightened voice, Jessica whispered, "Mother God, are you going to make me apologize to these people for passing out among their flowers and crushing some of the petals?"

"Trust me," came the less than reassuring reply. A middle-aged woman in a leather apron answered God's knock.

"Jessica," God spoke, "I want you to meet Heather. Heather, this is Jessica." She turned to Jessica. "Heather is one of the village healers." She then turned to the lady in the doorway. "Our guest, Jessica, is not used to drinking so much mead," God tutted. "Do you have any herbs or elixirs for her headache?"

Jessica let out the breath she was holding with a look of relief. "I really don't feel good at all," she told the Celtic medic.

"But of course," came Heather's reply. "This happens all the time around here, *especially* with some of these guys who claim to be seasoned drinkers."

God chortled to herself and backed up onto the path to leave. Heather invited Jessica inside, where there was a cozy fire in the hearth and a full wall of vials, jars and small packets. Heather poured a small mug of mead, "Start with some of the hair of that hound that bit you," she grinned. She then took some dried flower petals from one of the boxes and mixed them into the mead along with a drop or two of oil from one of the small vials. She gave the mixture a stir and Jessica could swear she saw smoke rise from the vessel.

"Drink this," Heather commanded. As Jessica lifted the mug toward her mouth she caught a strong odor that almost brought the berries she'd eaten for breakfast back up, but she drank the entire mug full and then took a deep breath. She was sure that she was going to be sick right there in the woman's cottage, but by her third lungful of air, her head was feeling much better.

"Wow," Jessica marveled. "What was in that? I can't believe…."

"Professional secret," Heather giggled, "unless, of course, you wish to remain here and study to become a healer yourself? It is an honorable trade."

"Back home in Israel, I'm supposed to *be* a healer. But I've never had anything quite like that!"

Jessica thanked the woman three times, still shaking her now much improved head in amazement. She was learning, bit by bit.

A few hours later, God found Jessica on the edge of town, humming a tune while the harp player strummed an accompaniment. Jessica looked up to see Mother God approaching. "Oh hi, Mother God. We were just rehearsing a new song I created, based on one of our old Hebrew melodies."

Mother God gave her a broad grin. "So then I suspect you'll be staying here for a day or two?"

"Well, just until we can perform my new song," Jessica told her. "It's called Hava Nagila, and it has quite a danceable beat!"

Mother God burst into laughter. "Yes, my child. You must remain here for another few days. The people of the East can wait for us!"

Jessica performed her new song with the pipers, harpists, whistle players, fiddler and a barrage of drummers pounding out the straight forward beat. The people danced to her song until late in the night. Everyone loved Jessica's tune, although many complained that they didn't get the simple rhythm. It was in four/four time, God later explained. The Irish dances relied on a much more complicated mathematical beat for the rhythm of their dances. Simplicity was good, but not always appreciated.

Jessica told God that after her performance, from which she gained a total understanding of the Irish music, she was ready to move on and see more of the world.

XXVI

Afold bidding goodbye to the Celtic village over round after round of mead, Jessica stumbled down the path to the beach. Mother God awaited her there, in her original dark Ella Fitzgerald style persona. "I hope you learned something here in Ireland," she said. "You certainly made an impression! I think we can count these people as faithful followers for the many generations to come! When the Romans bring your faith, these people will be among its most ardent adherents!"

Jessica bowed her head. "Mother God, I really feel like these are my people. I know I'm the savior of the tribes of Israel, but I feel such a strong bond with these Celtic tribes."

"Of course you do, sweetie. They…we are all your people. We are really all just one people. That's a part of what you are to learn from this trip through time and space. We are all God. We are one, we are all! There is no separation! Those who would separate themselves from their fellow Gods are the only true blasphemers.

Sleipnir appeared to boil up out of the calm sea, restlessly pawing the sand with three of his front hooves. He was anxious to continue their journey and stood stock still while Jessica threw a leg over. God just kind of drifted up without effort to place herself on the horse's broad shoulders.

"We've got a long ride ahead of us," God told Jessica. "We're going halfway around the world, so you might want to hold on to me and close your eyes. Try to get a little shuteye. We don't have any in-flight movie scheduled for this journey, so you won't be missing anything."

"In-flight movie?" Jessica's face was a mask of confusion.

"Just a little future humor, sweetie. Sorry. I keep forgetting where I'm at in time and space." Mother God reached back and squeezed Jessica's hand.

Jessica woke up briefly to see lush dark forests flashing by beneath them, then closed her eyes again. When she stirred once more, they were high over endless desert sands with a blue line of mountains rising in the far distance.

By now, wide awake and well rested, Jessica watched with fascination as the blue line on the horizon took a bumpy shape, then grew higher and higher before them. Sleipnir beat his legs harder as the air around them grew thinner and colder. Underneath them, snow blanketed the sharply defined rise of rock and earth.

And then they descended into a green valley hidden among the snow-capped rise. Sleipnir gently lowered them to the meadow, and two men in bright saffron robes with wispy white beards emerged from a cave in the mountain's side, running across the grass and waving a greeting to them.

Jessica and Mother God touched down and the men stopped their forward progress, bowing their heads and holding their hands together in front of their faces, shouting, "Nameste, Mother God, nameste! It is so good to see you once more! And this must be your daughter that you have created to save the world! It is such a pleasure that you have brought her to meet us and to share her company with us."

Mother God, still in her Ella persona, floated off Sleipnir and advanced toward the two Holy monks, holding her own hands together in prayer and repeating, "Nameste." She hugged both men in turn, then called Jessica forth to meet these men who accepted God for who she was, without pretense or local garb.

The monks hugged Jessica then backed up and kept grinning while they bowed toward her until God said, "Enough of this appreciation, already. Hey, Jessica is just like you, guys! You know that!"

The first monk stood tall. "Of course this is true but, Mother God, it is seldom that we meet someone with such a brilliant and open minded aura!"

"I have an open mind?" Jessica inquired.

"Of course you do, hon. How could you have anything else? But, listen. That's part of why you're here. So pay attention to these boys, you might learn something!"

XXVII

The two monks led God and Jessica back to their cave, where they had water boiling for a pot of strong green tea. The smoked some strong herb, drank the tea and talked about Jesse's life and the minor miracles she had learned to perform. Broad smiles never left the faces of the monks. They laughed upon hearing of her comedy performance to cure the lepers and her invasion of the money changers with yapping puppies. "And you should have seen when she restored the vision of two blind men by telling them she was standing naked before them," God giggled.

"But I guess I'm really here to learn from you," Jessica told them. The shorter of the two monks replied, "And we from you," bowing to her.

"One must never stop learning," said his partner.

"Knowledge expands as quickly as the universe around us," the short monk added. "The more you learn, the more you realize how much more there is to know. Let us share a meal as we think on this truth."

The first monk turned to a sort of barbeque pit in the rear of the cave and filled small bowls from the pots on the brazier. Returning to his seat, he handed Jessica and his partner the bowls filled with brown rice and small cakes made of bean curds. He sprinkled a bright orange powder on the mixture for additional flavoring. "It is a mixture of the roots of ginger and turmeric," he told her. They ate in silence, the two monks chewing slowly and savoring each bite. Jessica followed their lead and found the small meal very satisfying.

When the rice was finished, the diminutive monk announced that it was time to take a walk.

Somewhere in the past hours, God had left them. Jessica had been so engrossed in listening to these wise men, that she hadn't even noticed Mother God's departure.

The yellow robed men led her across the meadow and down a small embankment to the side of a rushing river. "Here before you is the primary lesson of life," the taller monk told the entranced girl. "Life *is* water! All the souls you seek to save are but tiny droplets of liquid in a stream much like this one. They flow through life, never touching the same place twice in their rush to the sea. Some will reach the sea more quickly than others," the old man smiled, twisting his long and thin white beard with his left hand.

"And the ocean," queried Jessica. "Is that the heaven where the good souls come to rest eternally?"

The second monk burst forth with hearty laughter. "If only it was that easy. No, young Jessica, if all our souls just kept pouring into the oceans, soon the oceans would overflow all the lands, even up to the height of this tall mountain. Flowing through a life is only a part of the cycle. Mother God has to *keep* the streams flowing, and so the souls that have washed to sea must evaporate and turn to a steam that can rise to heaven, where the clouds will bring them back over the land to let them fall again as gentle drops of rain, coming down to watery life and flowing for another round!"

Jessica rested her chin on the backs of her hands, elbows on her knees as she sat on a stout rock, watching her teachers closely. "From the ocean, the souls rise to heaven? Is that what you're saying?"

"Yes, that's part of it," the first Holy man replied pensively. "In fact, that's where your Torah legends got the idea of souls rising to the skies above, but they missed the true lesson of the cycle of birth and death, what we call Samsara. The cycle must complete itself by raining all these souls back to the earth and into the stream of life once more where they can put new energy into the ground and nourish all living things, plants and animals alike!"

"That makes sense," Jessica agreed.

"And another important law in the universe is balance. We call it Yin and Yang. What your people often mistake for good and evil."

"There is really no such thing as good and evil," his partner interjected. "Life just *is*…. What you call evil is the other side of good, just as pain is the opposite half of pleasure, or light and dark; so many things in life that are simply Yin and Yang.

"The pleasure you experience," the first monk told her, "is directly proportional to the pain you have suffered. If you never suffer pain, how could you know pleasure?" Both monks stood before the flowing stream with their beatific smiles.

"I think I get it," Jessica offered hesitantly.

"Of course you get it," said Mother God, emerging from a bubble between two small rocks in the water's depth. "You're no dummy, kid! Remember those temptations you went through after your long time of fasting? How good could food taste if you'd never been hungry?"

The two old monks gave God a quizzical look, then the smiles returned to their faces and they nodded their heads.

Jessica was confused. Had these men been with her in the cedars when she went without for forty days?

"They can tap into your memories," God assured her, patting her arm. "Remember, I told you we're all one? Someday you'll realize that you can get into other people's heads as well, I mean you're doing it already, but you just don't know what you're doing! How do you think you heal people?"

"I guess I never thought about it," Jessica said with a frown. "I was inside their heads?"

"Of course you were! Every living thing has the power to heal *itself*, but if he or she doesn't *realize* it, what good does it do them? Until a person is enlightened enough to realize he or she has all that power, they can't use it, but you come along, get in their head and *plant* the thought very deep that they have the power and *voilà*! They're all better. At least for that one instance."

Jessica shook her head violently to try and clear it, but mild confusion still reigned.

"From the largeness of our minds," the shorter of the two monks told her, "we understand the happiness of all men!"

"And from the generosity of our hearts," his companion grinned, "we each endeavor to promote it!"

"This is how it should always be," the short monk finished.

Mother God sat on the riverbank behind them, her legs crossed in a lotus position and her hands resting in her lap. Her eyes were closed and she had the sweetest expression of peace glowing all about her.

XXVIII

L ater, back in the meadow, Jessica took God aside for a heart-to-heart. "Mother God, I'm amazed that there is so much going on in the world while we Hebrew people have been wandering around one small desert."

"Oh, didn't I tell you?" Mother God wore a sheepish expression. "This isn't all happening at once. You and me? We've been traveling back and forth through time as well as space. You'll learn how to do this on your own pretty soon. From time to time you'll need to do this to speak to your people when they stray too far from the path!"

Then Mother God let out a deep sigh. "But it won't always do much good… that old Yin and Yang thing again."

"What do you mean, Mother God?"

"You can lead a horse to water, but you can't make him drink."

"Well, if the horse isn't thirsty…."

"Or doesn't realize how very parched it is," sighed God

Back at the cave, the monks invited Jessica to join them in an evening meditation. The taller monk bowed and introduced himself as Zhou, and his partner as Wen. Zhou and Wen… It almost sounded to Jessica as 'now and then,' but she didn't say anything.

After another meal of rice and bean cakes with some onions and green peas mixed in, Jessica took the proffered straw mat and joined her new friends in a deep meditation. She copied their posture as they sat in a full lotus position, just as God had on the riverbank.

When she came out of her trance-like state, Jessica found the setting sun to be much brighter than it had appeared to her before; the grass seemed greener and everything more well-defined. Jessica stumbled off to her pallet in the cave and fell into a deep, dreamless slumber.

When she awoke, Zhou and Wen were headed back out for a morning meditation before they prepared their breakfast. Jessica joined them again, which further heightened her awareness of the landscape surrounding her.

After a small meal, the monks once more shared their wisdom with her. They offered Jessica riddles and tales that they called Koans, short sentences designed to start her mind thinking deep thoughts. They laid mental puzzles before her, like what was her face before her parents had met and the sound of a single hand clapping.

Jessica found herself fascinated by these exercises. She anxiously awaited each new session with Zhou and Wen.

After a few days, the monks announced that they needed to go into the village.

"There's a village," Jessica asked. "Nobody ever mentioned a village."

"We have, of course, common people here," Wen told her. "It is our duty to see to their needs."

"Did you think there was just us in our, how do you say, ivory towers?" Zhou laughed. "Come with us! It will be a part of your learning!"

"These folks are no different from us," Wen assured her. "We don't think of ourselves as better or lesser, we are just, how would you say? More enlightened? More deeply aware?"

Jessica walked with Zhou and Wen along a winding mountain road for some hours, finally arriving at a cluster of bamboo and mud huts. Children in rags roamed the alleys between the dwellings and men loaded wood and grain onto ox carts in the narrow lanes. As they entered the town, the people all bowed to them and mumbled "Nameste."

One woman came forth to them holding a small boy with colic. Zhou touched the child's forehead, then assured the mother that the boy would be alright.

Farther along, they came upon a weeping woman. She told them her man had been slain in a senseless fight over a few beads. Zhou and Wen comforted her and assured her that it was God's plan, and a better man would soon come her way.

At the end of the day, the citizens of the village brought them a large bag of rice and a sack of fresh vegetables. They thanked the monks profusely for their guidance, and one of the town elders offered a ceramic jug of rice wine.

Jessica, Zhou and Wen sat with their benefactor at the edge of town and drank the potent spirits, sharing philosophical rhetoric and tales about someone they called the Buddha.

By the time that they returned to their mountain meadow, Jessica had decided that she must remain with these men to learn all she could from their simple, yet amazing life.

Mother God told Jessica she could remain if that was what she wanted, but there were other places they must eventually go, with differing lessons to be learned.

Jessica agreed with God that she should explore every culture that could teach her to better serve the people of the vast, wide world, but said she still felt there was so much to be learned here at the top of the world.

In the end, Jessica spent almost two years in Tibet. She learned about life from the monks and their studies. Zhou and Wen introduced her to other Holy men that traveled through from the lands they called India, China and Mongolia. Jessica and her mentors spent many months in these mountain caves exploring the Zen Koans, these riddles with very existential answers that led her to deeper thoughts about the structure of the mind world as apart from the physical. Jessica traveled through the transcendental labyrinth of thought, cause-and-effect; a land beyond the reality she'd grown up knowing.

With a broadly expanded consciousness, Jessica called upon God one day to say she was ready to move on, but that she must return to visit Zhou and Wen once more before she could return to Israel.

XXIX

This time, Mother God came to her on an Indian elephant, bidding Jessica aboard for what would be an extended flight over a vast body of water.

"This pachyderm provides a bit more comfort than a simple horse," God explained. "We'll be flying across the northern end of a great sea, along what was once a shallow land bridge, where the New World people were able to cross from the continent of the high mountains.

"Many of these New World people are the most kind-hearted and gentle in my flock."

"Many of them?" Jessica inquired.

God chuckled, "That Yin and Yang thing, sweetie. There has to be bad to balance the good, negative against positive. What breaks my heart is some of their tribes claim to be doing the bad in my name! They sacrifice their own *children* as they plead with me to bring them rain and a good harvest of crops."

Jessica gave a puzzled look. Mother God laughed. "It's all meat from the same bone," she smiled. "What can I say? You'll meet them soon enough and you can draw your own conclusions.

Their large gray ride launched itself into the night. Jessica dozed as they rose into the evening sky. When her eyes opened again, they were high above a tossing sea filled with what appeared to be large chunks of ice. Jessica watched in fascination as they transitioned from this turbulent sea to a mountainous continent of lush green. There were some fjords that reminded her of the land of the Vikings, but they soon advanced over the coastal rise to a broad expanse of green wilderness.

The elephant turned south, but continued on. These lush evergreen forests seemed to go on forever as they lost altitude. Before long, the elephant morphed into a horse. Not Sleipnir, the eight-legged Viking horse, but a large dappled brown and gray beast.

Their equine ride glided close to the ground and deposited them at the edge of a village of straw and timber dwellings. A dark-eyed lady somewhat shorter than Jessica came out to greet them. Although she didn't speak a word, Jessica received communication from the woman telepathically. The words seemed a bit odd, more like a poem than a greeting.

"See the delicate drop of dew
on the spider's silk
how it rolls from one end of the strand
to the other when the breeze is gentle?
Yet if there is no air to move it,
It will drop to the earth
To be absorbed
like so many thoughts falling into your head
And if the wind grows wild
causing tears in the silk
making it stand up or fall down like wild hair
that is, like all else, in natural order.
For you see, what you don't see
and hear what you can't hear

the nature of this world
is merely balance seeking to right itself.

"Yes!" Jessica exclaimed, understanding in an instant. "Another Koan; a Zen riddle!"

Jessica marshaled her thoughts to reply, but found it wasn't necessary. The New World lady smiled a smile full of love and acceptance. Then she actually spoke words. They were in a foreign tongue, but Jessica understood. The woman was welcoming her to this broad world of wilderness that belonged to every living thing. Behind the woman, others approached; men, women and children dressed in clothing made from the hides of moose and deer. Some wore the feathers of what must have been enormous birds in their hair. All appeared beatific and happy.

Jessica was offered a meal of roasted corn, squash and meat. She was hungry from the long night's flight and ate vociferously of the corn and squash, pushing the dead flesh to one side. The natives gave her knowing looks without judgment. When the meal was finished, they brought forth a pipe.

Jessica was expecting some heavy ganja and took a deep pull which sent her into fits of coughing. These people were smoking something very different from the good Middle-Eastern herb!

Her choking brought smiles from the men of the tribe, but no one criticized her unfamiliarity with their tobacco plants.

Jessica tried to explain about the Hebrew tribe into which she was born, about their rituals and beliefs. The New World natives only smiled and nodded. When she spoke of Moses and his ten commandments, a tall man with a head dress made of many bird feathers who was called Quiet Elk explained some of their philosophy to her.

"The sacred circle, having only one side, is everything," he told her. "Life, breath, birth, death and more. Because of its special shape, the circle is in perfect balance."

Yes, balance, Jessica thought. Yin and Yang, just as the monks and Mother God told me. In that instance, she understood these New World people and felt that she was one with them. There was still so much to learn! How could anyone ever be content to live and die in the arid sands around Nazareth!

"Like the sacred circle," Quiet Elk continued. "We must always be very aware of the oneness of all things."

Then the lady who had first greeted Jessica came forward. "I don't know how it is with your people, but we believe you must respect and honor your elders. I am known as Open Flower"

"Yes," Jessica told her. "Yes, Open Flower, We also honor our elders."

"We honor our elders," the woman told her, "because they carry the wisdom of the world on their backs!"

"I guess that's why we do to, although no one has ever expressed it quite like that...."

"We honor our children," Open Flower continued, "because they carry tomorrow in their hearts."

"I never thought of it like that," Jessica confessed. "But you are correct. Our children are our future, the future of our entire society, the whole world! Where would we be without our children?"

"This is why children should always be properly instructed about nature and the world around them. But above all, our children and we, ourselves, must honor all of the living creation! All the world around you is a gift, a very special gift that will insure our lives and our future. If we neglect any part of nature, we put *all* of nature out of balance. And when nature is out of balance, how can anyone within the circle grow and prosper?"

Jessica pondered this for a moment or two. All the New World people were silent as she gave the message consideration. Of course they were right.

"We must care for everything in nature," the woman emphasized. "Even the lowliest rock or stone. The stone people are just as important in the plan as we who stand on two legs!"

Jessica sat back to meditate on these new ideas. What could she say? Her own teachings never reached *this* far with all their worries about original sin, and guilt. Rocks and stones as people!

The New World people did not interrupt her thoughts. It was as though they could sense that Jessica was traveling back in her mind to find answers that might come from her own teachings.

XXX

As Jessica awoke from her meditation, the compact native woman called Open Flower was there before her. "You must know of the power of nature around you," she said. "Everything in nature has a role to play, a purpose in the scheme of life."

Jessica stared up at her with an open face and a waiting mind. How could she respond to this woman who obviously was just as in touch with Mother God as she was? It could only be disrespectful to give a reply!

"Are you in touch with all God's creatures?" the woman asked.

Jessica had no good answer. In touch with creatures? Was this some kind of trick question? Another Koan? Certainly she had *empathy* for the animals around her, that's why she didn't eat any meat other than fish, but in touch? Jessica had no idea how to answer this.

"Here in our boundaries," Open Flower told her, "we have many bears. The bear is a sign for introspection. He reminds us to look inside ourselves to find the answers to life's challenges. We must revere the bear as he is one of our great teachers."

"The bear is a teacher?" Jessica inquired back to her. "What about domestic animals, like dogs and cats?"

"Dogs symbolize misplaced loyalty," Open Flower told her. "You may have dogs, and you may mistreat them. They will still be loyal. They will keep coming back in spite of your mistreatment, always expecting that the next time you will be good to them.

"These dogs can be the most loyal of creatures, but a basic flaw in their character leads them to trust when trust may not be appropriate. We learn much about both loyalty and trust from the dogs that live among us and help us to hunt."

"And cats?" Jessica asked, "what of cats? The Egyptians keep cats as a sort of God… and I have some cats that I feed as well. Of course I don't even dream that I own them…."

"Cats are the most intelligent of animals," the woman told her. "They are a symbol of independence. Cats will always be free. One cannot own or possess them. If you are a good person, they will sense this and stay close to you. Cats always choose the humans that they want to associate themselves with. If you have cats that come to you, you must be a good and fair person."

"And what other creatures have messages for us?" Jessica asked. "What of these large birds that fly about around your village?"

"Do you mean the large birds with brown feathers and white heads? They are the eagles! We believe the eagle is the *symbol* of the creator of heaven and earth! While other birds may hide from the storms of snow and rain, the eagle soars *above* the storm, watching and protecting his domain! There is no other creature like the eagle!"

"And fish?" Jessica asked. "In my land we harvest many fish to feed ourselves. Is there a significance to the fish?"

"There are many varieties of fish," Open Flower told her. "Each individual species of fish has its own magic, if you could tell me the variety of fish?"

Jessica was at a loss. Fish were fish. One caught them, cleaned them and then ate them. Was one that different from another?

"The salmon that we often catch here locally," the native woman told her, "are a tribute to determination. Each year they swim upstream against interminable odds to spawn and lay the seeds for their young. The salmon are much revered!

"But at the same time, many of the salmon are yin to the other's yang..."

There was that yin and yang thing again! Jessica bent her ear closer to hear what the woman had to say.

"While so many salmon are very focused on swimming upstream to spawn, we also have the apathetics; the ones who procrastinate and never get beyond the mouth of the stream. There is much more to this fish story, if you would care to learn about it."

"Yes!" Jessica cried. "I want to know it all!"

"So then, are you familiar with the fish they call the dolphin?"

Jessica admitted that she had never heard of this fish. Could they be one of the fish she ate back home in Nazareth?

As though reading her mind, Open Flower continued. "The dolphin is found in the deep waters of the oceans. It is a large and very intelligent fish, maybe not even a fish at all, although it swims and looks like a fish.

"After the creator had finished making the universe and everything in it, she realized that the earth would need some kind of being to tend to it, to keep it healthy and in balance, so she conjured up man, who would walk on two legs, tend the animals and harvest all the bounty of fruits, nuts, seeds and other things."

"This is all very interesting," Jessica told Open Flower. "Our people have some silly story about the first man being born in a garden where he's forbidden to eat the most appetizing of the fruits."

"Your people could be partially correct with their story," the woman told her. "But to our story, there is more and it goes much deeper.

"Mother God laughed when she saw man, and said that this creature would never do. 'It has no claws or fangs to defend itself,' she smiled. 'And it has no fur to keep its body warm. How will such a thing survive the trials of living among the seasons and all the other creations?' So eagle, the creator, sent the wolf to talk to this two-legged beast. The wolf is a teacher... but the wolf is also a student. The wolf symbolizes a lifelong quest for knowledge. He lives among large numbers of his own kind as a family, and they help each other with tasks, like feeding the pack. Wolf taught man to seek the answers he needed"

"I thought the wolf was just another dog," Jessica voiced quietly.

"Oh no, the wolf is much more, so much more intelligent than dog. And we who walked on two legs learned from watching wolf, and we acknowledged wolf!"

"Fascinating!" Jessica exclaimed.

Open Flower laid her brightest smile on Jessica. "I think you are beginning to understand about the world, so I'll continue. When wolf understood that two legs had learned from him, he had eagle create the dolphin to be a messenger. Dolphin is also highly intelligent. He has answers and can grant two legs that which he needs."

"Dolphins talk to you?" Jessica looked quite amazed.

"Dolphin may talk to you in dreams as can all the animals, or they can just send you answers…. But, of course, sometimes you have to ask dolphin, let him know that which you seek!"

"But there is just so much to learn!" Jessica exclaimed.

"And in time, you may learn all that you must know for your life," Open Flower replied. "But above all else, you must always have unconditional love, like the love that flows from Mother God, and from the children. Unconditional love is the key to everything!"

"Children love as Mother God does?" Jessica asked.

"Of course they do." Open Flower assured her. "Children are all *of* Mother God. They enter this world loving all that surrounds them. They are curious about everything and they love each living thing they meet, until something hurts them or grown-ups teach them fear. From fear and the suspicions of their elders, children learn not to trust. When the children no longer trust, they begin to put limits on their love, conditions for them to accept what they don't feel they can trust. You must always keep in your mind and in your teachings that if you put no conditions on your love, there can be no disappointments in love!"

XXXI

When their dialogues came to an end, Jessica was ready to call on God to send her eight-legged horse, but the tribal elders told her it would not be necessary. The New World people had their own strong magic that could take Jessica anywhere she wished to go. Jessica requested that they might return her to the mountain tops of the Himalayas, so she could once again call on the wisdom of her brothers, Zhou and Wen. She desperately wanted to sound all this new knowledge off them, even though she understood down deep in her being that the New World people were descendants of the Asian dynasties who had crossed the one-time land bridge between the two masses of continent. All this wisdom came at some point from the same fountain.

The tribal elder, Quiet Elk, with all the eagle feathers on his head and trailing down his back, sat Jessica down in the large communal dwelling where dinners and ceremonies were held. Many of the senior members of the group were already gathered there, sitting cross-legged around the room's perimeter.

A young lady entered the room carrying a beaded leather pouch and proceeded to pass out organic, dark brown buttons from her bag. She radiated love and trust to all around her and, when she stopped before Jessica, their eyes met as though sharing a deep secret although the woman said not a word. Jessica took a couple of the fruity discs. She pocketed one and held the other in the palm of her hand sensing that this was what the New World people wanted her to do.

When the girl with the brown buttons had gone, Quiet Elk told Jessica, "These are from Mother God's most sacred cactus plant. We eat them in order to share God's wisdom, and to go places we could not reach simply walking, or on horseback. The sacred cactus can take you wherever you wish to go. Please, put it in your mouth and chew it thoroughly."

As Jessica chewed the small brown circle of matter, her vision burst into bright panoramas of reds, yellows, blues and greens. She found herself floating above the forests, so happy she could cry, but at the same time, so much a part of the universe there was no need to shed tears. She felt as though she might be sitting at the right hand of Mother God!

The others from the tribe hovered around her, their eyes aglow and a feeling of love so powerful pouring forth from them that Jessica could see it as a series of shining silver threads connecting them all as one. They once again communicated among themselves without words. Their thoughts traveled the strands of love that bound them together.

Quiet Elk bowed his head and Jessica could read unspoken words, telling her to meditate on her chosen destination and she would soon arrive there. He also wished her a safe journey, wherever she might travel, and let her know she was always welcome to return. To the people of the New World, she would forever be considered family. "If you wish to rejoin us at some future time," Quiet Elk told her, "you need only chew the second cactus button you have in your pocket."

Jessica bowed her head back to these wonderful people and then, closing her eyes, she picture Zhou and Wen in her mind. She saw them standing before their cave, but the photograph in her mind seemed much bolder and brighter than any reality. Patterns of energy seemed to engulf her as well as her old friends.

The next thing Jessica realized was another pair of silver life lines touching her heart. She knew deep down in her consciousness that these silver strands had now connected her to the two monks so far away. She drifted lazily along the connection, but as she soared above the vast sea below, she saw many strange visions.

Sea birds would fly beside her and speak her name. She could tell that they recognized her as a very special person. Whales and dolphins far below also looked up and paid their respect. Even the white caps on the ocean seemed to be speaking to her as they danced their merry dance. An undulating pattern of arabesques and paisleys seemed to play along the water's surface.

As Jessica, in her highly enlightened state, felt she was approaching the high mountains of Tibet, God appeared before her. "Jessica, wait!" she cried, "Listen, there is something I have to share with you before you leave the new world! I just love these guys! Maybe the best thing I've ever created. Come with me! We'll just take a brief detour through time."

Jessica didn't know quite what to think. Her head was already spinning from the powerful cactus button, but, as commanded, she detoured to follow Mother God, her head so full of love that anything she encountered would be universal love itself! She couldn't see them anymore, but she could feel that she remained connected by silver threads to Zhou and Wen.

Soon, Jessica found herself in utter chaos! There were so many bright lights and such large crowds of people, not to mention lines of some sort of chariots with glowing bulbs, bright white fore and red aft. The whole scene was mentally upsetting in her current psychedelic state. Jessica felt as though she'd been cast into some kind of vortex with no possible escape. So much conflicting energy everywhere around her!

She followed God into the largest building she'd ever seen amid screams and hollers from the crowd. In her experience, no one had ever shouted so loud at any of her sermons. Were these people all mad?

Then a hush fell on this mass of crazy people. Four young men walked out onto an elevated platform in front of all these dizzy souls. Someone in an amplified voice shouted, "The Beatles" and the crowd erupted in screaming once more. Some of the crowd appeared to swoon or pass out from the closeness of the mass of bodies. Then the young men began to sing, playing on some weird sort of stringed harps.

Mother God appeared to grow weak in the knees and clutched at Jessica to remain upright, eyes rolled back in her head. "Oh yes," she cried, "my very best creation ever!"

The four young men sang a few songs, nothing special in Jessica's estimation, but the mass of people went totally berserk, just as did Mother God.

"Don't you just *love* them?" God swooned.

"Well, they're okay, I guess," Jessica replied, not wanting to hurt God's feelings.

"You don't think they're the greatest thing you've ever heard?" God inquired with a disappointed face.

"To each his or her own," Jessica replied. "I'll give it a seventy-five, 'cause you can dance to it, but....

"Okay, alright," Mother God fumed, "Back to your Zen monks with you then. Last time I'll share *real* pop culture with you! Harrumph!"

XXXII

By the time Jessica reached Tibet, she was starting to come down from her peyote trip. Colors were becoming more normal and the swirl of patterns that danced had slowed to a weak pulse. Wen and Zhou were happy to see Jessica again, celebrating her return with rice wine and rounds of extemporaneous Haiku poetry. In spite of a night of drunken revelry, all three were awake, alert and ready for morning meditation the next day. Over rice cakes and tea, they discussed Jessica's coming return to her people half a world away in Israel. It was easily agreed that she was a very different person from the girl who had journeyed from her homeland some years ago, but the two monks assured her that this was all a positive thing.

"Everything happens for a reason." Wen assured her. "The universe is structured that way! And nothing happens by chance!"

"But everything happens by chance!" Zhou expounded clapping his hands together. "That is the way of the world!"

Jessica was momentarily confused, then she thought back to her Zen training, 'the sound of one hand clapping,' and she smiled.

"I'm just sorry to be at the end of my adventure," she told the men.

"But you are only at the beginning," Zhou grinned. "*Every day is a new beginning!*"

"I so wish I could take you back with me," Jessica replied wistfully.

"Oh, but you will!" Wen assured her. "There is still much to do and to learn! We have pilgrims who, as we speak, are preparing to venture down the mountains to the land of the Hindi. Maybe if you go with them, you can catch a caravan down what is called the Spice Road toward your homeland. You must never stop learning! In my meditations, I already see you among these people and offering them your help!"

"Spice Road?" Jessica said in wonderment. "Just what is this Spice Road?"

"The people of Rome and beyond? They have a great hunger for the roots and leaves that grow here in the East. They are willing to pay exorbitant sums to have these things to cook into their foods," Wen told her.

"They send traders to Cathy and India to secure these items they call 'spices'," Zhou added. "They brave great hardships; bandits, robbers and the harsh climate of the deserts. Those who succeed are rewarded handsomely, the others…."

"What a fascinating tale!" Jessica bubbled. "Yes! I'd love to meet these adventurers and travel with them. How do I go about meeting them?"

Zhou clapped his hands with glee and Wen bowed his head with a wide grin. "Arrangements have already been made," Wen told her.

"We knew this is what you would have wanted," Zhou smiled.

By the next dawn, Jessica had all her belongings together and was ready to start her journey home along the Spice Road across the great deserts of the Orient. They went together into the village, where a dozen men and women waited near the edge of the habited area. An old, white haired man stood before the group as their leader. He spoke of the hardships they might endure as well as the lessons they could learn from the Hindu people, who also had knowledge of the Buddha, people who were once one with them. The folks in the group nodded like sheep, more than ready to begin their trek down the rugged mountain side.

As they followed their leader, the path grew steep over the side of their wide plateau and onto sloping, moss-covered rocks. There were wide ravines cradling raging rivers, crossed by tenuous bridges of ropes and vines, some barely wide or strong enough to support their troop one person at a time. The views were spectacular, if more than a little frightening. At one point, Jessica saw the waters of the stream where she had studied the lesson of flowing jutting out so fast over the side of the mountain that it rushed straight forward from the rock wall for many yards before it curved gently down across the ravine in a spray of bubbles and droplets. And the path wound ever downward between walls of moss-covered granite and screed.

Along a very narrow ledge, one of the women stumbled on a loose rock and pitched forward over the side to her screaming death. Her husband let loose a pitiful wail and, for a moment, it seemed as though he might leap after her, but the leader held him back and comforted him, assuring him that it must be the will of the Master, exacting a payment for the good they might accomplish among the Hindu people.

It was a full three days downward climb before they landed on level ground, the highlands of what was known as India. Here the roads became wider and easier. There were even sign posts to guide the way, although they were written in Sanskrit and no one in the group could read them.

At the first large village they passed, Jessica asked around about caravans back to Rome or other Western points. Most of the local folks gave her a wide berth, but she finally found a man who knew something of the caravan trade.

This man, with a wide, white turban and flowing beard, directed Jessica to stay with her group until the third village up the road. "When you reach the town of Kashmir," he told her, "Go to the public market and ask for a man named Bagwan. Tell this man you have talked to Banamurti and he will introduce you to the fellows that run the caravans across the desert.

XXXIII

Jessica left the Tibetan troop at the outskirts of Kashmir. She didn't tell anyone she was leaving, just kind of hung back as they moved on. When the group was out of sight, she headed toward the center of the berg and the open marketplace.

Bagwan was easy to find. He had a stand in the market buying and selling teas. Jessica introduced herself, mentioning Banamurti's name. The man touched his finger to the side of his nose and nodded Jessica toward a beaded curtain at the back of his stall.

At the rear of the market, Banamurti had a small stand of camels tied to a bodhi tree. "We will be departing just before first light," he told Jessica. "It is unusual for a lady like yourself to be traveling on her own, with no male as a protector, but I have received instructions in a dream that you will be okay. Also, the fact that you are dressed in the yellow robes of a monk. I will stand as your protector if it comes to that."

Jessica laughed. "I think I can watch out for myself," she told him, "but your pledge of assistance is certainly appreciated!"

True to the man's word, Jessica was the only single woman traveling alone. In fact, there were only two other women in the caravan, both of them the wives of sultans hoping to capitalize on the high price of the spices they carried.

The train of traders traveled on the backs of camels. Camels pulled wagons full of jars and provided rides for businessmen and travelers alike.

Jessica had a camel of her own, not a real beast, but a conjecture of Mother God similar to Sleipnir. It had only four legs, but boasted the same magic powers as the Viking God's proud animal. She called her ride 'Bupkiss' or 'Bippie' for short and the camel proved to be her loyal consort.

The captain of the caravan, noting Jessica's saffron robes, granted her a narrow bed in the back of a yellow goods wagon with brass lanterns all around it. "I think your presence is a good omen," he told her. "Buddha will be watching over us!"

The caravan meandered on for endless days and nights. They came down from the highlands of northern India, then up the Khyber Pass and into Pakistan. A week later, they were crossing endless bleak desert, with little food or water to be found.

Just when the surroundings had them all feeling hopeless and depressed, when everyone thought it couldn't get worse, trouble struck.

Each night as they stopped to rest, two of the men were posted at the edge of their camp to warn of approaching strangers. Jessica, sleeping on her own in the back of a goods wagon, usually woke up before dawn and wandered out to perform her morning meditations in the peaceful surrounding sands.

On this particular dawn, Jessica sensed that something wasn't quite right. She couldn't seem to slow her thoughts and, opening her eyes from her failing relaxation, she saw two men stealthily creeping behind the caravan's guards. As the first man rushed forward to pull a scarf around the neck of the lead security guard, Jessica went into miracle mode.

She projected herself, larger than life, some twenty feet from the ground above the caravan and called in a stage-projected voice, "What is going on here?"

The highwaymen looked up, and seeing Jessica in her yellow robes hovering above, fell to their knees. Their eyes focused on the sand before them.

"We are sorry, dear lady." one man shouted.

"We are only trying to feed our families," called his partner. "Please spare us! We mean no harm."

"It looked to me that you were about to kill one of our travelers. That's 'not meaning harm'? And stealing the belongings of others? You have the gall to say you mean no harm?" Jessica thundered. "How can you say such a thing?"

"Robbing caravans is all we know," argued the first thief, a man of medium height with thinning hair and a mangy beard. "This is our life, such as it is!" He scratched at his facial hair.

"I do not wish to die in sin," screamed his partner.

Jessica remained silent for some time, thinking about how she should deal with these men. Finally, she came to a conclusion.

"You know that what you are doing is wrong?" she asked them.

"Yes, yes," answered the second man shaking his head wildly side-to-side. He was a younger chap with a thick head of wiry curls. "But we must feed our families."

"Well," Jessica smiled. "I may be able to grant you forgiveness. But you must learn an honest and honorable profession, one that does not put an unfair burden on society."

"But what else is there we can do?" said his balding partner. "We have no education or training."

"Can you read? And write?" Jessica asked.

"But of course!" the men answered almost in unison. "We are not simple riff-raff!"

"Then I will *grant* you a profession," Jessica told them. "You will be charged with helping the travelers that come and go on these roads, rather than stealing their possessions."

The two men gave each other looks of confusion and wonderment. "And how are we to do this?" thinning hair questioned.

"You will protect each traveler that agrees to accept your help. You will exact a sum from them, based on the value of the cargo they carry, against any tragedy that might come their way. You will write up a contract that you will call a 'policy.' If nothing bad happens, you may keep what they have given you. If they are robbed, or fall into other misfortunes, you will compensate them for their losses as specified in your policy!"

"But we will be forever paying out to these people!"

"Not hardly," Jessica laughed. "First, you know the other bandits. You can warn them not to prey on the people who are your clients. Beyond that, what percentages of caravans actually do get robbed? I think it is small and you'll do very well. Sure you'll be paying out to some of these people, but you'll be putting away a lot more of what you collect."

"And this will be a profession?" Curly asked.

"Of course," Jessica grinned, "You'll be... *insurance* men!"

Mother God materialized later behind Jessica's wagon. "Aren't they still stealing from these people?" Mother God asked her.

"Yes," Jessica told her, "but at least they're providing a service and giving some of it back! Now they have what will be a legally recognized profession."

"You're learning about this Yin and Yang stuff," God tutted with a wicked grin. "I think maybe you're learning a bit too well!"

"But of course, Mother God. You told me yourself that I'm a quick learner."

XXXIV

When the sun had risen and the caravan came to life for the new day, Baldy and Curly made their first sale. Hearing how close his little group had come to disaster, the captain of their caravan was happy to work out a contract with the former thieves that now called themselves insurance men and even promised to recommend their services to others he might meet along the dusty road. They would still post sentries at night, but they would also rest easier.

As the two former highwaymen sat counting their take, Jessica approached them and formally introduced herself.

"I am Akmed," the fellow with the curls told her. "And my partner is...."

"Patel," the other man smiled. "I am so happy that we have met you. I feel that this is the start of a whole new life for us."

"Yes," his partner bubbled. "Now that we have a profession, the other children in the village will not look down upon my small son and daughter. My woman may hold her head up with pride and tell everyone that she is the wife of an *insurance* man!"

Mother God, with all her knowledge of the future, looked down from above and shook her head. "I guess it had to start somewhere," she told herself.

As the weeks went on, the arid land around them grew greener and more hospitable, and they found themselves following the shores of a vast body of water. In Jessica's meditations, she perceived that she was more than half the way home.

The body of water they walked beside grew larger, eventually blocking their path as it twisted around to the north and they found a group of ferrymen that could load their beasts and wagons onto small, flat vessels to carry them over this inland sea.

Crossing this large expanse of blue-green proved a frightening experience for all, though the ferrymen assured their clients that they had made hundreds of crossings on this inland sea and were quite skilled at it. At times the wind would gust up so strong that it seemed it would capsize the craft while pushing her forward. At other times, the breeze would suddenly die down, and they would drift very slowly without sufficient propulsion.

More than once, Jessica rose up out of her body to hover above them and check their progress. Although she knew God wouldn't let them down, she found it reassuring to drift overhead and see their small procession of boats moving smoothly across the calm waters.

In two days time, the ferrymen were able to deposit them on the far shore and everyone breathed a sigh of relief. The captain told all the travelers that they would, in another week, reach an even wider sea, but they would not have to cross this next water. Soon, they would reach Constantinople, were they would go over a well-built bridge from Asia into Europe.

Jessica knew that she would have to say farewell to the spice train before their wagons reached that river. Soon, she would start inquiring in the villages they passed through about a road south to a place called Ankara. The Ankara trail would lead her across this land known as Turkey into Lebanon and more familiar surroundings. From Lebanon, Jessica knew her way home well.

XXXV

J essica approached the familiar banks of the Jordan River to find a very out-of-breath Mother God running down the road towards her.

"Jesse darling," God huffed, "wait up! Your learning journey isn't finished yet. Did you forget that we need to visit the library in Alexandria, Egypt?"

Reluctantly, because she was very homesick for her friends and family, Jessica followed Mother God across the Sinai. This time, they were ensconced on an ordinary jackass, so as not to attract undo attention.

"This place is gonna knock your socks off!" God told her.

"What are socks?" Jessica asked.

"My mistake," Mother God told her. "I keep getting unstuck in time. Socks come later. Anyway, it's just an expression. I mean this will, like, really amaze you, okay?"

"So, what's a library anyway?" Jessica asked.

"A library?" Mother God threw back at her. "A library is the most amazing center of learning ever invented! It's one single place, a repository or building where people store knowledge, in the form of books, scrolls and works of art. It's a collection of everything the people of earth know and understand, and it promotes the exploration of more knowledge. Kind of like the Koans you studied with Zhou and Wen promotes deeper thought?"

Jessica's look was totally perplexed. "I know of some scrolls in the temple, mainly the words of the Torah."

"Oh," Mother God moaned in a sort of ecstasy, "this is *so* much more. The works of the ancient ones stored in this library put the Torah to shame, if you'll pardon my saying so. Just wait until you experience it!"

Their little donkey was entering Egypt, although Jessica noticed that they also passed through a sort of wavy haze as they crossed the border from the lands of Israel. It was almost like she'd taken a small nibble of the New World folk's brown cactus button.

After another day of travel they arrived at a large, rambling complex of gardens and structures. Along the path through the complex there was even a small zoo populated with exotic animals.

"Long ago this place was dedicated to the muses," Mother God told her, "the nine goddesses of the arts. It's been a major center of scholarship from the time when it was first built many centuries ago. The library has collections of works along with lecture halls, meeting rooms, and gardens. It was once part of a larger research institution called the <u>Musaeum of Alexandria</u>, where many of the most famous thinkers of the ancient world studied."

Jessica stood in raptured awe. This so-called library was as big as many of the towns around Israel!

"The library was created by a guy named <u>Ptolemy</u>, a Greek cat," God told her, "who was really a Macedonian. Most of the books here are on <u>papyrus</u> scrolls. Scrolls made from a paper fashioned from the leaves of papyrus."

"Wow," Jessica exclaimed, "and to think I used to live just down the road from here when I was little."

"Actually, a lot of the library had been destroyed in a series of fires before your time, sweetie." Mother God told her. "We've just traveled back in time to before Caesar set fire to the main hall because I wanted you to see the place in all its glory. Impressive, isn't it?"

Jessica was speechless.

"In addition to all the books, the place had dining areas, a reading room, gardens, and lecture halls. Much like modern university campuses will have some day in the future."

University?" Jessica questioned, "What's a university?"

"It's a kind of school, but a very advanced school," God told her. "They won't have anything like it again for a few hundred more years, so you don't need to worry about such things. But it will be a very important place in the future. If you play your cards right, you might live to found the first such Institute of Learning."

As they walked among the massive shelves of scrolls, Jessica looked up. Just above one of the main shelves was the inscription *'The place of the cure of the soul.'*

"A cure of the soul?" Jessica asked gazing up at the lintel. "Of course," smiled Mother God. "Knowledge of life will *always* cure the soul!"

Jessica wasn't sure she quite understood, but she hesitated to question Mother God.

"The Egyptians are a very advanced civilization," Mother God told her. "I know your Hebrew people have some understandable prejudice against them as they once held you as slaves, but there's that unconditional love thing again. You can't judge everyone at face value."

Jessica nodded in understanding as God continued.

"The classical thinkers who studied, wrote, and experimented here include the greatest names of mathematics, astronomy, physics, geometry, engineering, geography, physiology, and medicine. People like Euclid, Archimedes, Eratosthenes and more."

Jessica didn't know any of these people, but understood that if Mother God was dropping their names, they must be pretty special.

"King Ptolemy wanted to have at least half-a-million scrolls in the library. They say that Mark Antony gave Cleopatra over two-hundred thousand books for the library as a wedding gift. Scrolls he had taken from the great Library of Pergamum. But you can't fool Mother God," she winked. "It was just a bit of propaganda meant to show Antony's allegiance to Egypt rather than Rome; Snarky politicians!"

"Mark Antony?" Jessica questioned, "Cleopatra?"

"Never mind, sweetie." Mother God patted her arm. "These are just more people in history that made a name for themselves among the unwashed masses. Not worth worrying about. Maybe someday I'll take you into the future. Someone in those advanced times will make a motion picture about Cleopatra starring Elizabeth Taylor!"

"Elizabeth Taylor?" Jessica queried.

"Sorry, another famous person in time you wouldn't know about."

"And what's a motion picture?"

"Well, how do I explain that?" Mother God appeared a bit flummoxed. "It's like a series of pictures that move… an imitation of real life, um, ah, well. Oh Jesse, I'd just have to show you one, if we get the time."

"They don't have any of them in the library? I'd like to see one right now."

"Well, not this library anyway," God frowned.

Jessica nodded, although she was still somewhat gob struck.

Mother God changed the subject. "When it was really rocking, this place was said to hold nearly half a million scrolls! All the ships visiting Egypt were obliged to surrender their books so they could be copied. The library filled its shelves with all the latest and greatest works in mathematics, astronomy, physics, natural sciences and some other things, like I might have mentioned before."

Jessica closed her eyes and thought about all this. She *did* understand what a scroll was and knew how important it was to have knowledge, to learn as much as you could in order to better understand the world around you. She smiled at Mother God and thanked her for the opportunity to learn about this strange place although she wasn't quite sure yet what it meant to her and her journey.

"But none of these motion picture thingies?" Jessica asked.

God cleared her throat loudly. Uh, no, uh, I don't think so."

XXXVI

L eft on her own to wander the stacks of this huge, ancient hall, Jessica began to realize just how special the place was. Healing herbs were explained, much like the New World people had shared with her. The astronomy section explained how the stars and planets moved, and how their gravitational pull could affect life in Jerusalem and other places on earth. The scrolls predicted the trine of planets that had, just after her birth, formed a bright star in the heaven that attracted the wise men, and how this particular formation would continue to appear in the sky every eight-hundred years, although it would largely be ignored in future time as the world soon would be accepting her as their savior. Much of the world, anyway.

There was just too much to digest in a single day, so Jessica rented a room nearby, returning early every morning for the next couple of weeks to explore the many areas within the vast complex of buildings.

There were giant maps showing that the earth was a round ball circling a star called the sun. These charts showed the separate continents that she had recently visited and the vast bodies of water in between. She was able to plainly see the location of the British Isles, including Érenn and the long peninsula where the Viking fjords were found just to the northeast.

Jessica read stories of the Greeks; about Plato and Socrates, and about mathematicians who broke the world down into complex formulas. She digested tales about brave warriors who sailed strange seas filled with monsters, sirens and mermaids, and she understood the symbolism of these strange tales.

When Mother God tapped her shoulder one day and told her it was time to return home, Jessica was years more mature in her learning in addition to the spiritual gleaning she'd brought back from her world travels.

"Scrolls here speak of an advanced race of people having very dark skins to the south and west of Egypt," Jessica mentioned. "Shouldn't we be visiting them before I return home?"

"These dark people were the first people to populate the earth," God told her. "The folks here in Egypt learned from the dark people. Much of the knowledge shared here is from these people, folks from lands called Kush and Aksum. But, unfortunately, these people have nothing new to contribute. What you know of the beliefs of the Egyptians pretty well sums up what there is to learn from the ancient societies of Africa."

XXXVII

ack on her home turf, Jessica quickly reconnected with her twelve disciple cats, hugging each in turn and telling them how much she missed their company. She was bursting to share all that she had learned on her voyage around the globe, but knew deep inside that they would have a hard time understanding, even as much as they trusted and respected her. Some of them might have a tough time just handling that the world was a round ball floating through space!

"Things have been going well here," Luke told her with pride. "Our followers have started calling themselves Crystians! And we're adding more to the fold each day!"

Jessica beamed at her little circle. "Well done," she told them, making eye contact with each man in turn.

But when she thought over all this news she had to share with them from her long journey, Jessica decided that she should probably go back to parables and fables to hip her buddies to Mother God's message. While she was musing on this, Thad asked her, "Who is the hippest cat in all the Voutesphere?"

School had just let out for the day and a crowd of kiddies were happening past them. Jessica called the children to her side. The kids were playful, happy and smiling. They exchanged knock-knock jokes and riddles with gleeful laughter.

"Just look at these happy children," Jessica told her twelve worthy studs. "Children may not realize that heaven is all around them, but they *are* in heaven and they get the most out of it! Kids are always *happening*; innocent and free. They love everything unconditionally. Their minds are open until grownups train them not to be so. They are curious and inquisitive. Yeah, verily, if you want to get the most out of life, you need to be like these happy kiddies! Only difference is that we adults have the ability to realize that heaven is all around us in the here and now!"

Peter nodded his head in the affirmative. "Yeah, I think I can dig it." And the others all made positive noises as well.

"Getting all hung up on the bad jazz in life is a life killer. Get all serious about things that don't matter to your coolness and you're gonna miss it, you'll miss so much of the joy and happiness that God has intended for you."

Her audience kept nodding their heads while the children went on about their fun. Some of the boys started tossing a ball around while others began a game of tag and they soon moved on.

"Yeah," Jessica mused, "if you are taking life too seriously you might as well hang a heavy millstone around your neck and take a long dive into the sea off a short cliff!"

"But the world ain't always all that kind to folks," Simon complained. "A lot of things happen that just aren't *right*."

"Woe to the world because of stumbling blocks," Jessica laid on them with a heavy countenance. "There's always going to be stumbling blocks, but if you step lightly, your fall won't be as hard. Just pick yourself up, dust yourself off, and start all over again," Jessica paraphrased from a song she'd once heard Mother God singing.

"It's like, say this shepherd has a flock of some one-hundred little lambs. One day, one of his little wooly bah-bahs cuts out for a walkabout, straying far from the fold. 'Cause the farmer loves all his charges, he knows he has to conduct a search for his young stray, leaving the other ninety-nine on their own for a few hours, or maybe even days until he can reunite their little brother or sister with the rest of the flock."

Simon tugged at his beard as he listened along with the others.

"Now when the shepherd dude find his little wanderer, like, he's gonna hug it and show it a lot of love. He'll feel more joy for his little lost one than for the other ninety-nine who just hung back and were cool, dig?

"And so it is with Mother God and all of her creations. She loves us all, but especially those of us who may have wandered into Never-Never Land, but then found our way home."

"Solid!" shouted Peter. "We're just like Mother God's lambs, *tres* cool!"

"Yeah, and dig this, like, if one of your buddy-cats does you a mischief or talks bad about you, bring it to this friend's attention *first*, like single-o and in private. By having a private heart-to-heart, you can get things straight between you without any, what should I say, embarrassment on either side. If this proves to get things mellow again between you, you've gained a solid brother!"

The twelve smiled at each other, then smiled at Jessica. "Yeah," beamed Thad. "Lay it down tight and right and then you got no need to fight!"

"Exactamenté!" cried Jessica. "I think you're getting my drift!"

"Alright," said Judas. "But what if the dude just keeps comin' on all salty and doesn't want to admit he might be wrong?"

"You might want to go back and confront the man with two or three witnesses," Jessica told him. "But if he keeps fouling the air with bad words, you probably want to lose the cat as a friend. At least Mother God in her wisdom will know you're cool. You can't let someone who wants to be a downer bring you down with them. Like I said before, heaven is all around you. Look for the good, praise it and enjoy it."

"But if you think this person spreading bad about you is a deserving, earth-angel type person, how many chances do you give him or her before you write them off," Matthew wanted to know, "maybe, like, a lucky seven chances?"

"Earth angel or the lowliest square," Jessica replied with a serious face, "give them seventy times seven chances! But at the same time, stand back so they don't spill the jam all over you!"

"I think I get it," Peter told her. "You just gotta keep the faith and try to see everybody's good side if they'll let you."

"Dig yourself," Jessica replied. "It's like some John has a lot of markers spread around town. He owes everybody, but especially, he owes this one money-lender dude big time, maybe like ten-thousand lire. The deadbeat cat wants to do the right thing, but he has no way to lay his hands on that much honest bread.

"So, like, he offers to sell himself to the cat, including his wife and children in the bargain too. They'll serve this guy like slaves until he can clear up what he owes. He actually throws himself down at the man's feet and promises to repay every single coin if he's given the chance."

"Wow, that's a pretty heavy load to haul," Luke murmured.

"Yeah, really," Jessica told him, but the money lender is so moved by the dude's offer, he decides to show some compassion. I mean, it isn't like he didn't have enough filthy lucre already. So he releases the cat and his family from servitude and forgives him his debt."

"A solid sender," Simon said. "Man has some true wiggage!"

"It's tres cool when people show their human side," Thad agreed.

"Yeah, but the man who is forgiven? He doesn't cop to the compassion gig so well. After all, he still owes a bit around town. So he goes to another buddy cat that owes him one hundred denarius and starts wailin' on the dude. Like, he grabs the man by the throat, very un-cool, and demands that the man pay him back immediately and in full!"

"I don't see a happy ending here," spoke Luke.

"And you are right," Jessica answered him. "The money lender hears about his forgiven friend's bad scene and calls him on the carpet straight away. 'Man, I forgave you some heavy baggage, baby, because you begged me and promised a show of faith. Now you're turning on some other poor dude and getting physical on *him* over some small change?' I mean the money man was really drug! 'Shouldn't you show some mercy on your own buddies just like I showed mercy on you? What are you thinking?' Then the money lender dude calls in some of his lieutenants and they wailed on the man until he begs once again for mercy, but this time he isn't shown any."

"Ouch," said Simon-call-me-Peter. "That's a serious lesson for the man to learn!"

"It is serious," Jessica told them all in somber tones. And the lesson is that Mother God says that when you forgive a brother or sister, you've gotta forgive them truly and from the heart!"

XXXIII

Jessica and her circle of twelve were steadily growing in popularity and found themselves booking more and more gigs laying down Mother God's wisdom for assemblies of common folks. They often played the seaside as well as market places and mountain tops. Everywhere they went, they were well received. Oh sure, there were a few hecklers in the audience from time to time, but her ratings were off the scale on the positive end and Mother God was pleased.

Jessica decided they would take the show from Galilee to Judea, across the Jordan River, and even there they were mobbed and did a large number of healings.

At many of the gatherings Jessica observed a certain Roman dandy staring at her from the first row or two. He was always well dressed in fur-trimmed, dark red robes with his black beard neatly trimmed and piercing ice blue eyes. And the man also appeared to be very into every word Jessica was saying. He had first shown up in Galilee, but tagged along with her entourage as they crossed the Jordan.

Jessica started asking around about this new fan. Some folks said he was connected in Rome; a gangster. Some others thought he might be gay. All agreed that he always seemed to flash a lot of cash around where ever he went. She learned that his name was Marion Mangelli, but everyone called him 'Made' Marion.

Rumor had it that when Marion Mangelli wasn't hanging at Jessica's little Chautauqua show; he ran the numbers racket around the area for a wealthy uncle in Naples. Jessica thought he was cute in spite of the rumors, even entertaining thoughts about winning his heart and trying to make him an honest man.

Finally, at an assembly outside one of the major temples, Jessica took a step into the crowd to heal a few children with colic. As she was laying hands on a thin girl standing close to Marion, she caught his eye and asked if he'd like to share a skin of wine with her later.

Such a wide grin burst onto 'Made' Marion's face that the little curls on his forehead seemed to be dancing. He hesitated a second or two, cleared his throat and said, "I'd be honored," in a musical baritone that made Jessica's knees go weak.

Jessica left the disciples to clean the grounds and pack up the show, disappearing round the corner arm in arm with Marion to where she'd seen a cozy little cantina that had ferns hanging in the big windows. It was a lovely, sunshiny day so they sat out front on the sidewalk. Jessica started to order the house red, but Marion put a hand on her wrist and asked the waitress to bring them the wine list. "I think you deserve the very best." He told Jessica adding, "I know a little bit about wine."

In the end, the owner of the small tavern brought up some dusty clay flasks from the cellar. When he'd uncorked the first, Marion held the vessel under his nose, took a long sniff, then closed his eyes briefly. "I think this will do nicely," he told the landlord slipping the man a handful of silver coins.

Marion and Jessica made small talk as the sun grew lower in the sky. She told him that she enjoyed traveling and had ventured far beyond Rome. She mentioned Zhou and Wen and the Celtic people.

Marion listened attentively to her every word, never once questioning how a beautiful girl could journey so far from home on her own. In turn, he told her about growing up in a marble palace beside the sea, and about the big mountain nearby his childhood home that always had smoke surrounding its peak.

Before they knew it, the second jug was opened. Jessica was feeling light headed, but she wasn't sure if it was the wine or the company. She found Marion a very interesting fellah besides being a solid shape-in-a-drape!

Candles were lit, more wine was poured and then the owner was staring at them, anxious to close the shop and take himself home.

XXXIX

Jessica woke up in an opulent room, silk curtains hanging over large windows, ornately carved furniture and 'Made' Marion's dark curls resting against her shoulder.

Marion stirred sleepily and brushed his lips against Jessica's. "So this is what it's like to make love to a Goddess!" he whispered.

"A goddess doesn't make love," Jessica smiled back. "A Goddess *is* love!"

Marion snuggled into her back and nuzzled Jessica's neck. They both sighed with contentment and dozed again.

Then Jessica remembered that she had a confab scheduled with her disciples for around noon. Embarrassed, she rolled over to face Marion.

"This was the most amazing night I've ever spent," she told him, planting a chaste kiss on the tip of his very Roman nose. "And I want to do this again, soon… And often! But I'm afraid I'm gonna have to split soon. I've got my ministry to oversee."

Marion laid a deep soul kiss on her. When he pulled back his face and tongue he told her, "I understand, baby. I got some things to tend to myself. Can I see you this evening?"

Jessica thought long and hard about her upcoming calendar. "This evening won't work," she told him with a sad face. "But Mother God knows where I can find you. I'll be in touch later today and we'll plan out our week. I want to spend every waking moment with you! Uh, oh, uh… I think I love you!"

'Made' Marion smiled back. "I wanted to say that first... 'cause I love you too! Really love you! And my dance card is totally blank right now. I just want to pencil you in on every slot."

Jessica got up from their bed. She didn't bother to pull her robe around her as she headed for the bath. Truth be told, she wanted to feel Marion's eyes on her, devouring her supple young body. Jessica had had a lover or two in her time, but no one had ever rocked her world like this. Her night with 'Made' Marion almost paled all her teachings and adventures around the globe.

XXXX

Although the love of Mother God had fueled Jessica and her ministry well for all these years, the love of Marion Mangelli put a bright new light into her eyes and an extra flash of fire into her speeches. The disciples all noticed the change. While they'd always maintained a professional relationship with their leader, some of them felt a touch of jealousy about Jessica's closeness to this half-Roman dandy.

Marion now remained nearby wherever Jessica went, carrying her scrolls for her and dusting off rocks before she could sit down on them. He was always ready with a word of praise whether Jessica healed one person or a full crowd. And, after each appearance, Jessica and Marion would leave together, the disciples knew not where. She no longer shared a skin of wine with the twelve to critique their sessions after the flock of faithful disbursed.

They couldn't find any fault with the way Jessica was doing her job. She was sharp and efficient in ministering, probably even more compelling then she had been in the past. In fact, Jessica was becoming so brilliant with her words that she was attracting attention from the people in power. The authorities now started seeing her as a very real threat to their hold over the masses and they weren't at all pleased.

Some of the Rabbis in the temple began seeking out the members of their temple that had been healed by Jessica's touch. They found a couple that had a teenage son who had been born sightless and asked if they could grill the lad about his experience with Jessica giving him back the gift of sight. They had heard rumors of two men many years before that had their vision restored by her and in these tales it seemed that Jessica had possibly used some kind of sexy hanky-panky in restoring their vision.

The parents agreed, after accepting a small bribe, and brought their son to the back door of the temple, where the senior Rabbi waited with a couple Roman soldiers in mufti.

"So, just how did this hussy go about making you see again," one of the soldiers asked the lad. "Did she promise you something about seeing her naked?"

"No, nothing like that," the lad replied. "She packed something around my eyes, something cold and clammy. One of the guys helping her told me it was Jordan River mud." The youngster nervously licked his lips then continued. "When she wiped the mud away, I experienced light for the first time. The world was really blurry at first, but after the lady mumbled some words over me, my vision cleared up. I could see the lady and she was something to see! Also, a gang of bearded guys were hanging around and there appeared to be some kind of African woman hovering in the air over their heads."

"Are you sure about this?" the Rabbi asked. "'Cause we think this chick is some kinda witch or something."

"Hey, I remember this all pretty good," the young man protested. "It was a Saturday afternoon and I was down by the sea with my parents...."

"Wait a minute here, Rabbi," exclaimed one of the soldiers, working on a clever frame. "The man just said that this Crystal woman restored his eye sight on the Sabbath! Isn't there some kinda Holy law against that?"

The Rabbi gave a perplexed look. "Now why don't you give glory to God, young man? We know this Crystal woman is no good. I think we need to banish her from the temple! Imagine the nerve! Performing miracles on the Sabbath!"

"So tell us again what happened, young man," asked the other soldier.

"Hey, my man, I already told it to you just like it was, with the mud and all that. What is it? Do you want to become a follower of Jessica Crystal as well?"

"Not hardly, Jackson," the Rabbi replied in a derogatory manner. "You might be a disciple of this crazy lady, but I choose to keep following Moses. Now there was a solid and God fearing chap!"

And with that, the soldiers grabbed the young man roughly and tossed him out into the street.

XXXXI

Meanwhile, Made Marion was so head-over-heels in love with Jessica that he started laying all kinds of presents on her. He bought her a closet full of robes and a couple dozen pairs of leather pumps and sandals, along with a collection of wide-brimmed hats to keep the sun from her dark, beautiful eyes. She returned home one evening to find Marion pouring over a catalog of expensive hand-crafted Roman chariots.

"Hey, baby," he asked with smitten eyes. "How about you pick out a chariot that I can buy for you and I'll purchase a slave or two to drive us around in style?"

"Oh, Marion!" she wailed. "Haven't you been listening to my sermons? We don't need a lot of *things* to be happy!"

"But baby, you know I'm just nuts about you. And I want everyone to see how I cherish you! I can get my hands on the long daddy green by doing a few favors for the *family*, and I want to spend it all on you!"

"Marion, sweetheart, money can't buy happiness… I know how much you love me, and I'm happy just knowing that we have each other…."

"But I want the whole world to see it, baby," Marion wailed. "I'm gonna dress you in style to show everybody just how much I care about you!"

"Dear Marion, it would make me much happier if we gave all these clothes and shoes to those poor folks that don't have proper footwear, or maybe don't even have a single nice outfit to dress in." Jessica let out a big sigh. "Don't you know that wealth brings its own burden to your life? It brings greed and avarice to surround you, and you know what Mother God thinks of these things. I see it so often, how the rich people always seem to want more and more...."

A hurt look crossed Made Marion's face. "But I just wanted to impress you, baby."

Jessica stood close to her man, taking the collar of his robe in her left hand and laying a big kiss on his distressed mug. "Lover," she told him, "you impressed me from the first time we met. I'm impressed by your intellect, and the tender feelings you have for other living things, for people and for small animals. And I would be much more impressed by the way you might share what wealth you might acquire with those less fortunate than us!"

"But baby," he protested.

"No buts about it," she told him. "Mother God says that it would be easier for a camel to pass through the eye of a needle than for a rich man to realize that he has heaven all around him right here on earth!"

"So no chariot?" he questioned, "and no slaves?"

"I'll be your slave," she giggled, "and you can be mine! And when you're through having your wicked way with me, we can take some of those fancy robes and sandals down to the poor box at the temple.

"Seeing the joy on the faces of poor ladies and gents who never owned such fine things before when they receive these gifts will make my extremely happy. I would love you even more if it was possible to love you more… but of course I love you so much already. Yes, I'd probably love you just as much if you *were* filthy rich, but that's because I love you from the bottom of my heart without any limits or conditions!"

Made Marion smiled down on her and Jessica noticed his eyes were moist. "Baby," he told her, "you're the ginchyest!"

XXXXII

As winter was quickly approaching and the temperature was dropping, the poor recipients of Jessica's cast off wardrobe were indeed happy to have garments that could act as windcheaters. Jessica only wished that she could multiply those robes as she had done with bread and fish but clothing, being man made and not from Mother God, was not such a simple item to deal with.

With the cooler season's approach came Hanukkah, the Feast of the Dedication. Jessica decided it was time to put in a guest appearance at the temple in the Portico of Solomon.

As they neared the place, Jessica sensed that the crowd was a tad restless on this day, so she told Made Marion it might be better if he waited out by the curb. A number of the members of the temple had recently been critical of her choice of a mate, or even that someone claiming to be the Daughter of God should have *a mate* at all!

As she entered, the local Jews surrounded her. They seemed to be sporting a serious lack of gruntle!

"Hey Jessica, how long you gonna keep us in suspense!" a voice from the crowd shouted. Another hollered, "Like, are you the Daughter of God for real or what?"

Right away, she knew she was playing to a tough crowd. Still another called out "Are you The Crystal chick or not?"

"Hey cats and kitties, didn't I already lay it on you as to my credentials? So you didn't believe me? Like, all these cool miracles and things that I do in the name of Mother God, shouldn't that be proof enough for you all?

"Maybe you lot just ain't, like, you know, my real and true sheep? My hip, loving, earth angel people, they hear my voice and they know me! And like, if you can't hear me, maybe you ain't hearing Mother God either, dig?"

But the teaming mass just wouldn't be placated.

"Why should we believe that God is a woman?" came another strident voice. "Moses said he saw God and God was a fellah!"

"Like, I laid it on you tight, right and outta site to hip you to Mother God, and about heaven being all around you if you just open your eyes to Mother God's wonder. No one can deny you God's graciousness!"

But as she spoke, one member of the mob picked up a small stone and flung it at her, narrowly missing her head. The others followed suit.

"Hey, come on, cool it guys," Jessica shouted. "I demonstrated a lot of good works to you and all your tribe. And I did this all in the name of Mother God!"

"We ain't stoning you for your good works," a red neck in the front row cried out. "We're throwing rocks at you for blasphemy! You're just a *girl*, and you want us to believe you're God? Fat chance!"

"But if you are hip to the good stuff I do, can't you just accept that it's Mother God working through me?"

In answer, the red neck and two of his buddies rushed forward and tried to grab Jessica by her robe. Being a thin and fit girl, Jessica was able to slip from their grasp and leg it down the hall amid a hail of stones to the main door. Fortunate for her, they were mostly bad shots, but one or two of the rock missiles connected painfully with her back as she ran.

Marion, hearing the commotion in the temple and fearing for the worst, had hailed a cab. He had the tail gate open at the back of the hired chariot, dragged his Lady aboard by her shoulders and told the driver, "Put the pedal to the medal, Max. I'll pay any speeding tickets you might get."

Marion had the cabbie head for the Jordan River, having in mind that they might cool it in the place where John the Baptist had been pouring water over Jessica's followers when he was alive.

When they arrived by the Jordan, Jessica and her man were well received. The people around that river were true believers, many from the time when John the Baptist had lived there and had told them many solid stories about the Lady, Jessica Crystal.

XXXXIII

Jessica's twelve swingers picked up on the word that she and Marion had gone on the lam to the River Jordan and, one by one, they left town to join her there. Thad had suggested they should be cautious and blow the city separately so as not to draw any of the angry temple folk to their leader and the others agreed that this would be prudent.

While they were hanging out around the waterfront, the word came that the brother of two of Jessica's favorite girlfriends had been taken ill, a cat named Lazarus. Jessica remembered the whole family fondly. She recalled that one of the sisters, Martha had offered her a kind of kinky spa treatment that included the chick's drying Jessica's feet with her hair after giving her a very sweet pedicure. Having her pedal extremities dried in the woman's wig had been strange, but she kind of dug it. And Martha was Mary's sister. Mary was a very with it chick. While Jessica didn't know Lazarus that well, she figured anyone of their kin had to be aw-*reet*.

But for reasons known only to herself and Mother God, Jessica decided to just cool it by the river for another day or two. It was just a kinda funky gut feeling that she had. On the third day, Jessica told Marion that it was probably time to head back to Judea.

"Are you nuts?" Made Marion asked her. "Last time you showed your face there they threw rocks at you! At both of us!"

That sentiment was enforced by the voices of her disciples, but Jessica told them Mary and Martha were close compatriots and she felt it was worth taking the chance to give some comfort to their big brother, Laz.

"I heard he's fallen asleep," she told her entourage. "I'm gonna happen on down there to see if I can't wake the cat up."

"Sleep is cool," Simon stated, "a good couple days dozing in bed is a sure-fire way to heal the man's illness."

Jessica gave them a troubled look. "Fellahs, ol Laz ain't just snoozin' like that. The man is seriously dead!" which brought a few gasps from the group.

"Okay, so we'll go and we can die with him," joked Thomas. "Somebody was sayin' that the man has already been in his grave for a day or two."

"The family lives in a little berg called Bethany," Jessica shared. "Marion, you know the way there?"

"Sure, baby," Made Marion smiled; it's just a hop, skip and a smidge outside the petticoats of Jerusalem."

A large number of Jews had gathered at Mary and Martha's pad bringing condolences and prayers. Knowing that there was some hostility between the people of the temple and Jessica, Martha parked herself at the city limits sign to wait for the Lady and her special followers.

Mary stayed home entertaining the troops. Martha, meanwhile hung it on Jessica that if only she had been there, Brother Laz might still be alive and kickin'. "But I can dig," she told Jessica, "that, you and Mother God being tight and all, whatever you ask of the Godly Woman, she'll probably let you have your wish."

"You know your brother will live to ride again," Jessica assured Martha with a wink.

"I know he'll rise up when Mother God has her judgment day," Martha smiled.

"Judgment, smudgment," Jessica told her. "We all judge ourselves in this veil of tears. And if we're hip to the jep, we can give ourselves high marks, leave the tears behind and start enjoying all the wonders that surround us without any judgment!

"I'm here to hip everyone to the fact that they can be, in a sense, reborn into the bigger, brighter world of unconditional love, God's love. Do you believe this? Can you feel the power?"

Then Martha did a singularly peculiar thing. She took a pigeon from her robe, attached a note to its foot that announced, "The teacher is here and we're headed your way." She held the bird above her head, and the pigeon took off in the direction of the house where Mary waited.

The bird arrived quickly, as the house was nearby. Mary coaxed the bird to her hand with a few crumbs of matzo and unfolded the small square of parchment from its skinny ankle. When she'd read the missive, Mary took off post haste and many of the Jews who had come to mourn with her followed, thinking that she was probably heading to the cave-like tomb where Brother Laz rested.

As soon as Mary reached the crossroads where Jessica waited, she wailed, "If you had been here my brother probably wouldn't have copped the grim reaper scene!"

This accusation stung poor Jessica. She was deeply moved by Mary and her entourage of Jews, some of whom had been ready to throw rocks at her only a few fortnights before.

"So where did you lay your brother cat out?" queried Jessica. And one of the Jews turned quickly saying, "Walk this way, great Lady and we'll take you there. And Jessica wept. Like, real tears because although it was a tragic scene, it was helping to overcome some of the people's doubt about her.

But one of the redneck Jews chuckled. "If this Lady could give eyesight to the blind, why didn't she prevent our buddy, Laz, from dying?"

At this remark, Jessica walked a little faster, up to the tomb, which was some kind of cave, its opening blocked by a huge boulder. Sure glad none of them is strong enough to pick this baby up and toss it at me, she thought to herself.

"Okay, Martha, can you get some of your tribe to roll away this rather cumbersome stone?"

"But Jessica," she cried. "It's been four days! The pong from that cave will probably knock us all down! Haven't you ever been exposed to dead flesh before?"

"Didn't I tell you that if you believe God will handle the small shit?"

So a couple of the laborer types put their backs to the boulder and shifted it far enough that the cave's mouth was partially exposed. Jessica gave a wink heavenward and mouthed, "Thanks, Mother God!" Then she stuck two fingers in her mouth and gave a loud, crude whistle. "Hey Laz, baby," she shouted. "You in there? I need you to come out here and tell these people who I am."

Lazarus stumbled out in a bit of a daze. He still had white, mummy-style tape hanging from his hands, arms and legs, and he had a handkerchief tied over his nose and mouth.

"Will somebody please pull that funereal garb off my friend and let him go?" Jessica called out.

Lazarus shook his head to momentarily clear some of the cobwebs of a couple days resting in a deathlike trance. "Jessica, baby!" he cried out. "I knew you'd come for me, you and Mother God being tight like you are!"

Then Lazarus reached both hands out toward the crowd. "You folks all know Jessica Crystal, don't you? She is the real and true savior, sent by Mother God to bring new life to our people!"

And the gathered Jews all shouted "Amen."

XXXXIV

Most of the assembled Jews were pretty chuffed up at this little wheeze and fell down before Jessica, pledging their support of her and her ministry. But a small, doubting handful went away to the Far-Out Sect folks to tell them what this naughty girl had done.

The insecure chief priests with the Far-Out Sect sent out word to assemble a council, the message asking, "What the Fuck are we supposed to do? This crazy chick is showing too many of the signs. Like, she is posing a true threat to our power! If she keeps this up the Romans are gonna come marching in to take away our land and our nation!"

But this one priestly cat known as Calloway, who had been named High Priest of the Year by Rabbi Magazine, told them, "You boys don't know shit! And you don't seem to cop to it that we could use a very vouty sacrificial lamb. This Jessica woman could be our best friend chick. Like, she could be wasted for the people so that the entire nation doesn't have to perish! Hey, it's not what I might want, but in my position as the priestly poll winner, I can dig this as a solution."

A lot of heavy religious heads nodded in his audience. The assembly was digging his thoughts, and it looked good to them.

"And not just for our little tribe," the Highest of High Priests told them, "but also to reach out and, like, send a sign to all the children of God wherever they might be."

And in the days after this clandestine meeting, Jessica had a price on her gorgeous dark head. She knew in her heart of hearts that she could no longer walk openly among what she thought of as her own people. She was forced to gather her disciples and lead everyone to a small stretch of wilderness where they could hide out. Fortunately, one of Made Marion's uncles owned a small fishing resort in a small rural berg called Ephraim and he offered them individual vacation cabins at off season rates.

They passed a few months at Uncle Guido's resort, but Jessica knew that Passover was looming large on the calendar. The Far-Out Sect knew this as well, and they started laying out bets on Jessica. Would she show up for the feast?

The High Priest of the Year and his Far-Out Sect buddies decided to put out the word. If anyone might know where Jessica was hangin' out, they should contact the High Priest Hotline where they might even get a one hundred lire reward. The Far-Out Sect were just drooling over the prospect of arresting Jessica Crystal for their own evil ends!

XXXXV

Six days before the Passover, Jessica and Marion decided they might pay a call on Martha, Mary and Lazarus, whom she had brought back from the big sleep.

Although she normally had trouble boiling water and ate out most of the time, Jessica called on Mother God to help her prepare a simple meal for Lazarus. Jessica boiled the pasta and Martha served while Laz reclined at the table sipping from some very cool grape.

"I'm sure you're not used to standing in the kitchen and cooking for folks," Mary said to Jessica when the spaghetti was served. "How about I give you a little foot massage?"

Jessica was digging it at first, but then Mary started pouring all this massage oil over her feet. When Mary started rubbing her feet with her hair, Jessica got upset.

"Hey, baby," she told Mary, "I'm an open minded gal, but what's with this kinky hair-rub business? Like, the whole place smells of this sex-shop ointment stuff!"

And her buddy, Judas Carrot Top commented, "Wow, what a vouty fragrance! Where can I buy some of this? Can we hand some of this oil out to the po'folks?"

Of course, Judas could care less about the fragrant oil or the po'folks. He just wanted to get under Jessica's skin.

"Don't put Mary down," Jessica told Judas. "She's just tryin' to please. She might just be practicing for the day I die, for all I know. Dead feet definitely need a bit of tending. There'll always be po'folk, but you won't always have me here with you."

Of course the word got out that Jessica was back in town. A whole herd of Jews started showing up on the steps, not just to hassle Jessica but also to see Lazarus, the cat that had, according to local gossip, risen from the dead. Lazarus's miracle recovery was a big reason why many of the Jews had started believing in Jessica Crystal.

And of course, Jessica took advantage of her new found acceptance. She walked out from the house and stood on a large rock to address the large assembly of her people.

XXXXVI

It was really one of Jessica's finest sermons to date. She hipped the gathered masses that Mother God soon planned to exalt them all to a throne of glory. That, with her help, Mother God would bring all the various nations together as one, and then God would be separating the sheep from the goats, so to speak, revealing who she knew to be pure of heart and giving of the unconditional love she's been teaching.

"And while those of you who are hip to the jep and love your neighbors just like your own will sit at God's right hand and experience all the many joys of this groovy, koo-koo world. You old goats who don't get with it will make another trip through the cycle of birth and death so Mother God can give you one more chance to grab that brass ring and say 'I can be anything this time around.'

"Cause, like all you righteous daddies, when you saw me hungry, you laid some of your own grub on me and shared your goodies. And when I was thirsty, you uncorked a really jivey bottle to slack my thirst."

Jessica paused here for effect, running her lovely eyes over the crowd and smiling.

"And when I was naked, you laid some fashionable threads on me. And when I was feelin' under the weather, you laid some medicine on me and came to my aid." Then she gave a wicked wink. "And when I was in prison, you sent me that very vouty loaf of bread with the hacksaw blade baked into it!"

And several in the crowd shouted out to her, "Jessica, baby, when did we see you hungry or thirsty or naked? Like someone locked you up girl?"

And she answered them all. "Like, whenever you did this for any of your good brothers or sisters, you did it for me because we are all one, we are God! To do for your fellows is to do for me *and* to do for Mother God!" And the crowd sent up a jubilant roar.

When the noise died down, Jessica put on her serious face. "But the bad news is, children that in two days the Passover will be upon us. And the word on the street is that the authorities are planning to silence me. Be forewarned!"

And not but a few blocks away, some of the civil servants were gathered with the 'old school' priests hatching just such a plot. The majority favored seizing Jessica by some sort of ruse or craftiness and then putting a knife in her back. But the cooler heads in the circle counseled that they would be best to wait until after the feast of Passover because if they made their move on the Holy day itself they'd be exposed as a bunch of non-religious rabble. One couldn't be too careful in these matters. If they played their cards right, they might even enlist the local governor to book the troublesome woman for a crucifixion or something!

"How about we advertise for someone who can hand this naughty girl over to us? It really shouldn't be one of our lot seen to be fingering her." said a temple scribe. "I can write some pretty compelling copy. Maybe even offer a small reward?"

The vote was all in favor of this man's skullduggery and the word went out that same afternoon. By nightfall, they'd actually attracted one of Jessica's own, Judas the Carrot Top, who agreed to deliver his boss to them for thirty large coins, "but make sure it's good Roman silver," Judas told them. "None of this questionable local mint tat!"

XXXXVII

Now, as the day of the feast of flatbread was upon them, the disciples all asked Jessica what the evening's plan should be. Jessica said she was open, "But let me talk to Marion," she told them. "He might have some suggestions."

That afternoon, as Jessica and Marion were having a little siesta cuddle, she asked Marion what he could suggest. Not being Jewish, Marion didn't put much stock in Passover, but he dug that it meant a lot to Jessica, so he gave it some thought.

"It should be the finest place we can get into," Marion assured her. "Especially if you think this might be your last supper in town. Why don't you let me talk to your boys about it and we'll get a plan together.

At Made Marion's suggestion, Jessica's friend Saul booked them into the ritziest supper club in town to dine, understanding that this might be the last time they'd all be able to get together. Jesse and her entourage walked down the high street to the nightclub, but they were met at the door by a very officious looking Roman dude.

"We've reserved a table for thirteen," Disciple Johnny told the man.

"I don't know," the maitre d' told him. "You cat's look Jewish to me. This is a class establishment. We don't serve *Jews* here.

"Oh for Crystal's sake," Luke exploded. "Do you know who you're dealing with?"

The stone faced doorman just stared down at him in silence. Finally, the club owner came down the stairs to survey the situation accompanied by Jessica's beau, 'Made' Marion Mangelli.

"Hey," he told the doorman, "these people's money spends just like everyone else's!" Then out the side of his mouth he said, *soto voce*, "Put'm in the back room, away from the high rollers. We got a reputation to maintain."

A busboy was still setting the table as they entered the rear banquet room. Jessica beamed at Made Marion and said, "The crease you ironed into those pants is so sharp you better be careful not to cut yourself!"

A titter ran through the disciples causing Marion to blush a bright crimson. Jessica put her right hand to Marion's left cheek and kissed his other. "Sorry, boyfriend, I didn't mean to embarrass you, but you *do* look really fine tonight."

"When all of the twelve were reclining comfortably around the table, Jessica whispered something into Made Marion's ear and Marion left the room.

He returned a few minutes later with a local boy that shined the shoes of the wealthy patrons at the club. Marion tipped the lad with a couple brass coins and asked if Jessica could borrow his box with its rags and polishes for about fifteen minutes. The boy gave him a questioning look, but then he bit down on one of the coins and realizing it was the genuine article, he smiled and pushed his kit over toward Jessica and went to stand in the hallway by the restrooms.

"So, chaps," Jessica announced, "while you all say a few words to glorify Mother God's name, I'm gonna give each one of you a really hot shoe shine. Simon-Peter, put those penny loafers of yours up on the box. You're first."

"Jessica," Simon-called-Peter laughed. "You're not really gonna polish our boots and shoes, are you?"

"That's just what I plan to do," Jessica told them with a solemn face. "I'll shine all of your footwear then you can shine my sweet little flats." She snapped the rag loudly over the toes of Simon Peter's two-tone loafers. And when she had finished each of the twelve in turn and all their shoes gleamed in the candle light, she laid it on them.

"Now you can all be confidently passing out wolf tickets all over town, and you should all feel proud and cool.

"But not all of you, 'cause one of you, and you know who you are, is gonna be siccing the law on me before the sun comes up. Those glowing ground pads are going to prove an embarrassment to one of you!

"The rest of you cats, do you understand what I have done?"

"You snapped a mean rag over a very vouty bunch of spit shines," Luke said. "Very cool," Thad added.

"You call me teacher and Lady," Jessica laid on them with a wink. "After I'm gone, I'll expect you to keep each other's ground pads lookin' spiffy all the time. I'm setting forth this little example because I want you all to remember that the slave is no better than the Master, nor the one who is sent any better than the sender. Everyone is equal and we *all* have to care for each other without any questions or embarrassment. When you know what's right and you do what's right, and you love everyone without conditions, you are truly blessed."

Eleven of the disciples were grinning ear-to-ear checking out the way their shoes were gleaming, but at the end of the table, Judas Carrot Top appeared a bit green around the gills.

"You who would break bread with me but then kick me down with your well-polished boot, you know who and what you are, as it is written." Her eyes moved over the assembled guests, resting on no one in particular, though she noticed that Judas had sweat dripping out of his red hair and running down his pale face.

"Yeah and verily, I say to you all that on this night I will be betrayed… but enough of this pity kick, I see the waiters are heading our way with some loaded down trays. Let's eat!

In spite of the club's anti-Semitic stand, they baked a pretty decent unleavened bread, and Marion made sure they got a jug from the top of the wine list. Only the best for Jessica!

Jessica grabbed a deflated loaf when the waiter set it down and started tearing it into bite sized chunks that she passed to each of the members of her party. "Hey, guys," she told them with a grin. "Think of this as eating a small part of me. With this bread, I share a big hunk of the wisdom I've acquired through my life and travels. It's like, a kind of psychedelic thing. Man, this bread is gonna make you high like you've never been high before!"

They all partook of the bread, chewing it into mush then looking back at her with glassy eyes.

"And this Dago red," she told them, passing the freshly uncorked flask down the table, "think of this as my blood! The blood of God's messenger, flowing through each of you, to give you all the magical powers of Mother God herself."

Eleven faces in rapture nodded a positive in unison while one made a small choking sound. Then a voice from the doorway shouted, "Yeah? And what about me, baby?"

"Hey, come on in, Marion, and join the party. I was hoping you could be with us!" Jessica beamed a broad smile at her half-Roman boyfriend. "But you've already tasted my body... And you know I've got you in my blood, big-time!"

Made Marion pulled up a stool next to Jessica, gave her a kiss on each cheek and sat, putting a possessive arm around her shoulders. He looked around the disciples for anyone that might challenge his closeness with God's own daughter.

Marion helped himself to a big cup of the wine. What the heck, hadn't he been the cat who recommended it in the first place? He ate a small piece of the Passover bread as well, but soon signaled the waiter to bring him a fresh, crusty Italian loaf with some balsamic vinegar and olive oil.

As they finished their bread, Jessica embellished on the disturbing news that one of her inner circle was going to sell her out to the cops soon, if he hadn't already. Each of her disciples in turn swore it wasn't them, but she gave them all a knowing look. The guilty party knew who he was, and that was what mattered.

"This is a really rough riff!" barked Matthew, but Jessica just smiled back at him.

"The path isn't a straight line," she told him. "It's more like a spiral. You just keep coming back to the things you thought you understood and, **voilà**! You start to see deeper truths!

XXXXVIII

fter the wine and the grub, Jessica announced a special treat. She had heard that a hot new group would be making their debut performance tonight on the club scene.

Unnoticed by the crowd, four of her disciples moved away from the table, heading toward the men's room in the hall.

Jessica promised a great evening of entertainment with her own Fab Four, the BeatleJews!

As she spoke these final words, four of her disciples walked onto the center stage. They were unrecognizable as they wore long black robes, wide brimmed black hats and dreadlocks over long false beards, looking as orthodox as hell itself.

Without further ado, they began shouting, "She loves you, Oy,oy,oy."

Jessica couldn't contain herself and almost fell to the floor with laughter until Mother God shimmered down with a very sour look.

"You think this is funny?" she demanded, ears steaming and face red enough to stop traffic on any major thoroughfare.

"Yes," Jessica screamed. "Yes! I do!"

"Oy," God screamed, "What have I created! I tell you I love these Beatle guys somewhere in the future and this is what I get in return?"

"Yin and Yang!" Jessica guffawed. "What goes 'round, comes round!"

God collapsed in a heap. She didn't know if she should laugh or cry, but then she thought about Jessica Crystal, the one God-like creature she had chosen to represent her point of view to the common world, and she had to laugh along… Uncontrollably!

As God looked up, the four were chanting a line toward the one of Jessica's disciples who had been chosen to betray her.

"Hey Judas, don't take it wrong,

You were meant to go out and get her

Remember that somewhere deep in your heart

You simply had to help them get her."

When Mother God approached the stage, the four pulled off their hats and dreadlock wigs with big grins.

"The Beatle-Jews," the master of ceremonies shouted, "Ringo Star of David, Johnny Leninstein, Paul McCartshwein and George Harrisman!"

"You're mocking me, sweetie! It's not nice to mock Mother God!" God reached over and gave Jessica's cheek a long hard pinch followed by a little pat. "Bitch," she whispered so only Jessica could hear.

Jessica flashed a big wink. "Oh, I think we're cool," she told God. "Then to her flock of twelve, she said, "Let's blow this joint. The place is a real downer!"

At the back of the room, Judas was shaking so bad that the thirty new pieces of silver the cops had put in his pocket were jingling like sleigh bells.

IL

The disciples followed Jessica through some olive groves to a knocked out jazz den called Gethsemane's Garden of Jive. She motioned Made Marion to her side, he put an arm around her and tagged along as well.

Knowing time was growing short, Jessica decided that she needed to trust at least one of her disciples to get hip to what the future might hold. She decided her old buddy Simon-call-me-Peter was the man she could trust, her oldest and dearest student. Just to keep things copacetic, Jessica let Peter know that before the dawn, he would need to deny her three times. After that, she slipped him a note asking him to meet her in the men's room at the back of the bar shortly so they could discuss future plans.

Once all the disciples were seated up close to the stage, Jessica announced that she really dug this cat, Luigi, that played a mean scat ram's horn and she wanted to go back stage to talk to him for a minute or two. About the same time, Peter excused himself to hit the gents.

Made Marion had booked a local belly dancer as the opening act, and the stripper did a great job of holding everyone's attention as Jessica and Peter drifted from the main hall. They met up by the club's rear entrance and entered the men's bog, where they locked the door behind them for privacy. Jessica proceeded to tell Peter that she knew the local gentry had been plotting against her for some time.

"They're sending out a squad of goons in the morning to arrest me for, like, unreligious behavior against King and country, or some such trumped up charges," she told him. "It won't be a pretty sight," she went on, shaking her head. "But Mother God is going to be looking out for me. The plan is these thugs will nail me up to a big Star of David on the hill and it will look like they're killing me, but God will do her thing to keep me safe and I'll meet up with everyone back here in a day or so."

"What a stone drag!" Peter lamented. "Are you sure you'll be alright?"

"We have to trust Mother God," she replied. "God says if she can make it look like I beat death, more folks will start paying attention to what I've been saying about peace and loving your neighbor."

Their dialogue was interrupted by a knock on the door. "Is Jessica in there with you?"

"No, man," Peter shouted. "I'm just feeling a bit ill. Give me a few more minutes. I think maybe the olive dip was a bit off."

They paused a few seconds to be sure no one was listening at the door, then Jessica told her friend of her plans to retire somewhere far away from the Middle East with Marion. "I'm tired of this crazy life constantly under the microscope of local Rabbis and Roman rulers alike."

Jessica was trying to explain to Peter why she felt she had to get away, when they were surprised by another loud, persistent knock.

"Hey Pete, you seen Jesse?" Luke's voice begged. "We can't find her anywhere. Man, like, we're really worried! That musician guy Luigi said she never went backstage or talked to him. I mean, like, there's rumors that the government might be out to get her."

"She ain't here, okay?" answered an irritated Peter. "Can you just give me a few minutes of peace?"

Jessica went on with her story. Like the Beatle Jews had sung, Judas was destined to toss her to the cops and then this crucifixion wheeze would happen.

"Judas is going to try and hug me or something to let the authorities know it's me. But," she assured Peter, "it won't be as bad as it sounds…"

The third round of pounding on the door was the most intense yet and accompanied by the deep baritone of Made Marion. "Alright, asshole, is my chick in there with you? If she is, I'm gonna have to do some serious ass kicking! And if I can't put a hurt on you, I got some guys on my staff that can!"

"No, no man," a frightened Peter called out. "What would I want with your chick?"

"Just watch yourself!" came Marion's reply.

L

Mother God briefly froze the scene so Jessica could climb out the window and Peter could walk out and resume his place at the table as though nothing had happened. Jessica strolled into the club a few minutes after that. "I've just been out in the olive groves behind this crazy juke joint praying." Jessica told them.

They stayed for the second set. Luigi let Marion sit in with the group to sing his favorite number, **Volaré**. On the next break Jessica suggested they head out for a little fresh air, but as they proceeded to walk into the starlit night a gang of local gendarmerie approached from the center of town. Looking behind her, Jessica noted that they had the street blocked to her rear as well.

Then Judas walked out of the cluster of officials. He came casually forward, grabbed Jessica in an intimate embrace and laid a deep soul kiss on her.

Made Marion exploded, bursting forward to punch the betraying disciple's lights out, but officers of the law subdued Marion while their buddies slapped the cuffs on Jessica.

"Hey, even the Romans wouldn't crucify a lady!" they heard someone in the crowd proclaim.

Then came another man's answer, "No, they'll just farm it out to the Sicilians. Those turds will do anything for a buck!"

And in the sort of frenzy that arresting cops will sometimes fall into, they punched poor Jessica then they beat her with clubs and socks filled with desert sand as they dragged her off to a holding cell.

There were so-called priests along with other supposed solid citizens parading around outside the city lock-up. Among them, Peter recognized some of the money changers turned pawn brokers and corrupt temple officials who were on the take from their parishioners, but two-to-one they were all outnumbered by the king's government officials who feared that a "Kingdom of God" might try to wean them off the taxpayer's tit.

LI

At first light, Jessica was brought before the king's governor, Pancho Flyboy, a man who feared everything around him that he couldn't control or subjugate.

Pancho racked his tired brain for the worst offenses he could think of; anything which might excite the crowds to a lynching! He desperately needed to render a death penalty on the chick so she couldn't get a good lawyer and appeal her case, which might drop him deep in the doo-dah!

"So you claim to be the King of the Jews," he sneered at Jessica, "but you're a *girl*! How does that work?"

Jessica stood tall and silent before the man, a beatific smile on her face.

"And you claim that God is an overweight African woman?" A titter ran through the crowd.

"But I've seen her, she is!" cried Judas, now a bit sick at heart that he'd sold Jessica out for thirty silver coins. Thirty silver coins! Hardly enough to buy a decent falafel plate and a bottle of Roman red wine.

Judas stepped forward and threw the purse full of Lire in Poncho's face. "I don't need this shit!" he shouted and the marshals grabbed him as well.

Jessica later learned that Judas had been so drug at betraying her he had hung himself in the cave where they parked him, using the belt from his robe as a make-shift noose. What a drag! He'd proved a pretty decent kisser!

Come the dawn, Jessica learned that to add insult to injury, they expected her to drag her own Star of David up the mountain! Well, at least she'd kept herself in shape. But when they marched her from her cell, there were only two pieces of the Star set out for her to carry.

"Give thanks for small favors," she told herself as she shouldered her burden.

Soldiers along the route snapped whips at her as she walked! Thank goodness Mother God had given her some dynamite shit to smoke and placed a spell on her so that she was feeling no pain!

When they reached the peak of Calvary Hill, Jessica looked around to see who was bringing the rest of her Star of David, but saw only a couple common thieves dragging wood of their own.

In a bit of quick thinking, Jessica remembered the small brown buttons the New World people had given to her when she'd visited them. Checking the pockets on her robes, she found the one remaining cactus disc she'd been saving all these years in case she wanted to return to the New World folks. She popped the disc in her mouth and began chewing as she saw God shimmering up the hill towards her.

"What's the deal, Mother God?" she whispered.

"Oy," God fumed. "You just can't get decent help these days! I *specifically* told them you should be hung on a Star of David! These lazy contractors, cutting corners with a simple cross beam. What kind of symbolism is this for the Hebrew people? I don't know what to say! The contractor tells me lumber is in short supply and we'd just have to make do with this! I don't know what kind of message such cheapness is gonna send to our people!"

God had to do a quick disappearing act as a couple Sicilian soldiers approached with nine-pound hammers and what *looked* to her like railroad spikes... but they couldn't be that as railroads were another eighteen-hundred years in the future.

God gave Jessica a wink. A minute later, the world lit up in bright colors and began to move in interesting patterns. Jessica looked up at the soldier taking her left arm to nail it to the crossbar. With her other hand she reached out and pinched his cheek.

"Bless you, handsome," she told him with a seductive smile.

"Wha? Lady, are you nuts? I'm about to drive spikes through your delicate little hands and feet!"

"Yeah, bummer of a job for you," she answered. Then just before she withdrew her spirit from her body, leaving an empty husk attached to her by that familiar silver cord, to be nailed to the crossbar, she wiggled her nose and the soldier smashed his thumb with his large hammer. The man sent up an ear-splitting howl and Mother God's voice told Jessica, "That wasn't very Crystian of you!"

"I just couldn't resist," Jessica grinned.

Jessica's spirit sailed over the crowd and sat down next to God, toward the back of the audience, to see what would happen next. She could not believe how soldiers and citizens alike seemed to delight in tormenting the lifeless portion of her that hung from the cross. Someone had placed a crude crown fashioned from knarly Hawthorn plants around her brow. A couple soldiers poked at her with spears while others gathered under the main post to sneak a peek up her robe! And it was all happening in glorious Technicolor thanks to the magic cactus plant.

From time to time, at Mother God's urging, she would project her voice, like a ventriloquist, toward the dying form atop the hill. Once she cried, "Forgive them Mother God because they ain't got a clue what they're messing with!"

Another time, she heard one of the thieves that hung on the crossbars beside her body moaning a lament about never seeing the Kingdom of God as he had been condemned and would die as a thief.

She turned the head of her dying body slightly to face the man. "Take heart, my brother," she consoled him. "The Kingdom of God is within you. Thou art God!"

A brief smile tried to reach the man's lips as he heard her re-assurance. In that instance he understood that she was indeed the savior sent to the Jews. Her remark also earned her a smack across her thighs from one of the soldiers tormenting her.

Later still, she called on some Holy cat named Elijah from the old tales saying, "Hey, Eli man, I'm thirsty up here. Could you send up a taste?"

"I never could stomach execution scenes," Mother God whispered to Jessica at one point. "I'll be glad when this little charade is over!" Jessica just smiled her beatific smile. If only God knew how she was tripping! But then Mother God must know! Wasn't she omnipresent and always hip to the happenings?

Throughout the drama, Made Marion had been locked away in a cave cell of his own. He heard distressing news from the guys coming on shift at the changing of the guards, but he also trusted in Mother God to keep his little heart-throb safe.

By the time they released Marion, the show was all over. Some rich cat named Joseph from out of town had collected what was left of Jessica's hot little body and announced he planned to put it in a cave and seal the cave with a stone. Some of the better soldiers kept a close eye on him, suspecting he might be a necrophiliac.

LII

Marion called on Jessica's mum, Mary to give his condolences, but as they chatted, Mother God appeared to cut them in on the plan.

"I know all about your scheme to run away with Jessica to Gaul," God told Marion, "and you have my blessing! I also know that Jessica is carrying your child, and I made sure no harm came to the baby throughout this whole dog-and-pony show."

Marion, normally a really macho, won't-see-me-crying kind of cat, fell to his knees with damp eyes, thanking God over and over again.

"Day after tomorrow, they'll roll away the stone and find an empty cave. I've got some fireworks and mass hallucinations planned to make them think Jessica has flown away to this imaginary place they call heaven in their legends, even though we all know heaven is all around us right here. It'll make great copy for the press! Probably make some serious history as well, though I'm not sure if that's a good thing considering how historians tend to screw up the facts."

Behind God, Jessica walked into the room. "Jessica!" Marion cried. "My love! I'm so happy to see that you're okay!"

"When you warm other people's hearts," Jessica told him, "you remain warm yourself. When you seek to support, encourage and inspire others; then you discover support, encouragement and inspiration in your own life as well. I just wish I could have made more people understand this!"

"Some will," God told her. "More everyday as time passes, but many will never accept it." God let loose with a deep sigh, "That old Yin and Yang thing again."

"But surely my disciples will document all that has happened. The world will read of this and good will win out over evil."

"Yin and Yang," God repeated. "Actually, in a few hundred years, your followers will convince the world that you were really a man… that it's a man's world. Some guy named Paul is starting this perversion of history as he pretends to be your biggest fan!"

"No, Mother God, this can't be!"

"But hey," God sighed. "We had a pretty good run at it, didn't we?"

LIII

By the time all the shouting was over around Israel, Marion and Jessica were miles away. They'd traveled to Alexandria disguised as pilgrims, where they booked passage on a boat under assumed names. Marion's cousin, Frankie had some connections in Gaul and he helped them secure a little place near the south coast overlooking the Mediterranean Sea. Jessica was able to retire in peace, far from all the Crystian versus Jew rhetoric that was rocking Rome. Marion claimed to be retired as well, but he still occasionally performed some 'favors' for the 'family.'

Jessica gave birth to a daughter of her own soon after arriving in Gaul. She named the girl Mary to honor her own birth mother. Mother God insisted that she should be the child's Godmother. Within two years, Marion and Jessica also had a son that God jokingly called "the true Son of God." With tongue firmly implanted in cheek, they called the lad Jesus.

Many of Jessica's followers got word of her escape and made the journey to Gaul to be near her. A large Crystian colony blossomed along the Mediterranean.

Jessica and Marion were able to grow old, leading a happy and blessed life on their south facing beach surrounded by Jessica's true believers. Jessica told Mother God that she was no longer interested in time travel although God kept egging her on, telling her that at a time way in the future there would be a big film festival on the very spot where she was now hanging out, Cannes, the place would be called in the future. Jessica couldn't quite get her head around the concept of 'moving pictures' or film, but she nodded at God and joined her two small children as they built sand castles on the shoreline.

ACKNOWLEDGEMENTS

I owe a big thank you to the Unity Church of Rockport, Texas, for guidance about the New Testament of the Bible, which I know only from speaking with Christians, not being one myself.

I also owe a big debt to Rebecah Hall, my Native American sister, for so much assistance in describing the indigenous people of America, their ways and beliefs. Becah shared with me the poem Jessica Crystal received telepathically from the New World people in Chapter XXIX and so much more about Native American culture!

Also, a big thanks to Carrie Roberts for posing as JC on the book cover. And thanks to Carrie's mother, Sheila 'Reetz' Rogers, for allowing me to exploit her daughter as our savior.

And again, thanks to Theresa Feeser, possibly the world's greatest editor.

ABOUT THE AUTHOR

Skoot Larson is a native Los Angelino, a musician, music critic and a Viet Nam veteran. He has also worked as a disc jockey, actor, speech therapist, stand-up comedian, behavioral counselor and streetcar conductor. His previous works include the Lars Lindstrom Zen-Jazz Mystery series, a black-humor novel about health care in America entitled "Apollo Issue," and a political humor novel, "The Palestine Solution." Skoot lives with his two cats in Rockport, Texas.

Made in the USA
Charleston, SC
28 March 2016